THE RISING SUN

Recent Titles by Robert Jackson from Severn House

DESERT COMBAT
FLAMES OVER FRANCE
FLAMES OVER NORWAY
FORTRESS ENGLAND

THE RISING SUN

SUN

Robert Jackson

severn
House

This first world edition published in Great Britain 1999 by
SEVERN HOUSE PUBLISHERS LTD of
9–15 High Street, Sutton, Surrey SM1 1DF.
This title first published in the U.S.A. 1999 by
SEVERN HOUSE PUBLISHERS INC of
595 Madison Avenue, New York, N.Y. 10022.

British Library Cataloguing in Publication Data

Jackson, Robert, 1941-
   The rising sun. - (The secret squadron series ; bk. 3)
  1.   Great Britain. Royal Air Force - Fiction
  2.   World War, 1939-1945 - Aerial operations, British - Fiction
  3.   War stories
  I.   Title
  823.9'14 [F]

  ISBN 0 7278 5414 3

All situations in this publication are fictitious and
any resemblance to living persons is purely coincidental.

Typeset by Palimpsest Book Production Ltd
Polmont, Stirlingshire, Scotland
Printed and bound in Great Britain by
MPG Books Ltd, Bodmin, Cornwall.

Prelude

Malaya, December 1941

For two days, the monsoon rains had been sweeping across the Malay Peninsula, the water falling in sheets from the clouds that rose in leaden banks from the roof of the jungle. The rains lashed the surface of Kota Bharu airfield into stinking mud and danced in an explosive mist on the tarpaulins that shrouded the engines and cockpit canopies of the thirteen Lockheed Hudson bombers of No. 1 Squadron, Royal Australian Air Force, standing squat and silent on the flight line.

No. 1 was one of three RAAF squadrons which had been rushed to Singapore in the summer of 1940 to form part of the air defence of Malaya against the growing threat of Japanese expansion in South-East Asia. Australian defence planners rightly considered that Australia's security depended largely on the maintenance of Singapore as a strong base, and the offer of an air contribution to the Malayan garrison had been readily accepted by the British Government. Yet, when Japan signed a ten-year military, political and defensive pact with Germany and Italy – nations with which the British Empire and its Commonwealth were already locked in bitter conflict –

1

on 27 September 1940, the Allied staffs were forced to admit that in the event of a war in the Far East, which now seemed a strong possibility, the ability to hold Malaya beyond the immediate vicinity of Singapore Island was problematical and that the survival of Singapore itself for any length of time could not be guaranteed.

A year later, when war with Japan seemed imminent, No. 1 Squadron had been ordered to its war station at Kota Bharu in north-east Malaya. Its primary duty was general reconnaissance and sea attack, with the bombing of land targets a secondary role.

The squadron had been the first RAAF unit to equip with the American-built Hudson, and the aircrews were well content with it. Modern and relatively fast at 255mph, it could carry 1,400 pounds of bombs and was armed with up to seven machine guns. RAF Coastal Command had already been using the type for two years, with considerable success.

The Japanese had been sending reconnaissance aircraft over the Malay Peninsula since early in October 1941, by which time No. 1 Squadron had begun its own series of reconnaissance flights out to sea, the Hudsons ranging up to 300 miles from Kota Bharu. By 1 December, reported Japanese troop movements in southern Indo-China, together with the rapidly deteriorating state of Japanese-American relations, had convinced the British Commander-in-Chief in the Far East, Air Chief Marshal Sir Robert Brooke-Popham, that the moment had come to bring all the forces under his command to full readiness.

It was not before time. On the morning of 6 December, taking advantage of a sudden and unexpected lull in the monsoon, three of No. 1 Squadron's Hudsons took off to carry out a sea search of three different sectors off the north-east coast of Malaya. Two of the aircraft reported nothing; the third, piloted by Flight Lieutenant Ramshaw, encountered what appeared to be half the Imperial Japanese Battle Fleet, 265 miles due east of Kota Bharu and apparently heading directly for it.

It was 1230. Ramshaw identified a battleship, five cruisers, seven destroyers and twenty-two transport vessels and at once radioed for permission to shadow them. This was refused and he reluctantly turned for home, his rear gunner reporting the course of the ships until they vanished behind a curtain of rain.

What Ramshaw had seen, in fact, was not a battleship but the heavy cruiser *Chokai*, flagship of Vice-Admiral Ozawa. There was another cruiser, too, the *Sendai*, and twelve destroyers, not seven. In the prevailing weather conditions, the mistakes were easy enough to make. It did not really matter. What did matter was that the transport vessels – there were in fact eighteen of them – were carrying nearly 27,000 troops of the Imperial Japanese Army's 5th Infantry Division under the command of Lieutenant-General Matsui, and that the whole force was heading for the coast of Malaya.

During the remainder of that day, and most of the next, the Australian crews tried in vain to relocate the Japanese naval force, the Hudsons flying in the most appalling weather conditions. The sea approaches to Malaya were almost completely hidden under a blanket of low cloud, rain and fog.

Somewhere beneath that grey curtain were the Japanese. By this time, the Allied staff in Singapore had no doubt that the Japanese meant to attempt a landing, but as yet there was no indication as to where that landing would be. An invasion of Malaya would mean all-out war between Imperial Japan and the British Empire, but a second option was open to the Japanese; it might be their intention to launch a sea-borne invasion of Thailand, in which case the outbreak of hostilities with Britain and her Allies might not be inevitable.

The search for the Japanese went on. Late on 6 December, a long-range Catalina flying boat – a civilian machine, flown by an Australian airline crew and impressed into service by the Singapore authorities – also took off to look for the ships. It never returned. The Japanese remained undetected, and in Singapore feverish preparations for war continued on 7 December.

It was now thirty hours since Flight Lieutenant Ramshaw had first sighted the naval force, and since then there had been no further reports. At Kota Bharu, frustration was intense. There was simply no way of knowing what the Japanese intended to do, and until they made their move no action could be taken against them. They held all the cards.

Suddenly, just before midnight on 7 December, there was news. Wing Commander Davis – No. 1 Squadron's commanding officer, who was in conference with Army Brigade Intelligence at Kota Bharu – received a report that four small vessels were moving along the coast from north to south, close inshore. Davis at once ordered one of his Hudsons into the air to drop flares and photograph the ships. Shortly afterwards, its crew reported that the vessels had turned sharply away to the north and were heading back up the coast towards Thailand.

The Hudson returned to base. Its arrival was followed by a tension-filled lull that ended abruptly at 1300 hours, when Japanese transports were seen lying at anchor off the coast and British coastal defence batteries opened fire on them. The escorting Japanese warships replied immediately; the first shots of the war in the Far East had been exchanged, but soon their echoes would be eclipsed by events far to the east, on the other side of the International Dateline. Shortly before the sun rose on what promised to be a beautiful, sunny Sunday morning, the first of 276 bombers and torpedo bombers, escorted by eighty fighters, were beginning to take off from six aircraft carriers of the Japanese First Naval Air Fleet. In a few hours' time they would be sweeping down on an unsuspecting Pearl Harbor, the Hawaiian base of the United States Pacific Fleet.

The gunfire along the coast could be clearly heard on Kota Bharu airfield. Within minutes, Wing Commander Davis received an urgent call from the Army, saying that Japanese vessels were anchored off the coast and that a landing appeared to be imminent. Bluntly, the Army wanted to know whether the RAAF could provide air support while the invaders were repulsed. Davis told Singapore what was happening, and quickly received orders to attack the enemy ships with all available aircraft. Some of the Hudsons were already bombed-up and the first of these, piloted by Flight Lieutenant Lockwood, roared away from Kota Bharu at 0108 and disappeared into the inky darkness.

Lockwood had no difficulty in finding the scene of the action. The darkness over the coast was split by the flash of gunfire, and drifting flares gave the whole picture a stark, nightmarish quality. Crossing the coast at 2,000 feet, Lockwood soon located the Japanese transports. There were three of them; the remainder, it later turned out, had headed northwards to carry out separate landings in Thailand, at Singora and Patani.

Lockwood pushed the Hudson's nose down and streaked over the lurid sea at fifty feet, heading for one of the Japanese vessels. Anti-aircraft fire lanced at him from all directions but he held the Hudson steady, releasing two bombs and then jinking away from the streams of tracer. His rear gunner reported columns of water rising close to the ship.

Turning, Lockwood brought his aircraft round for a second attack, curving in to drop his second pair of 250-pound bombs. The fire from the escorting warships was intense and the Hudson was hit again and again, but once more the pilot kept the shuddering aircraft on course and tore through the holocaust before the welcome 'clunk' of the bomb-release gear gave him the signal to twist away to safety. This time, the jubilant rear gunner shouted that both bombs had struck the transport amidships. A column of flame lanced up into the night, then died to a dull red glow as the Hudson sped for home.

The second Hudson to attack was not so lucky. Taking off at 0218 and piloted by Flight Lieutenant Leighton-Jones, of Melbourne, the aircraft was shot down flaming into the sea. Not until much later was it learned that this aircraft had carried out a fiercely determined attack, even when damaged and on fire, and that its bombs had severely damaged a second enemy transport.

The third Hudson to come roaring down out of the night was flown by Flight Lieutenant Ramshaw, who had been the first to sight the invasion fleet. He made his attack without seeing any dramatic result, managed to avoid the worst of the flak and returned to Kota Bharu, where ground crew worked feverishly to re-arm his aircraft.

The fourth pilot, Flight Lieutenant O'Brien, who took off at 0220, made a near-perfect attack approach, selecting the biggest of the three enemy transports. He pressed the bomb release – and nothing happened. Hauling the bomber round he made a second attack, thundering low over the ship and raking its decks with machine-gun fire before jinking away over the sea, pursued by meshes of tracer.

After a lull of fifty minutes, the Australians came back. This time, two Hudsons – flown by Ramshaw and Lockwood, making their second sortie – attacked simultaneously. Lockwood dropped his bombs and got away, but Ramshaw's aircraft never returned. For nearly four years, its fate was to remain a mystery. Then, late in 1945, Ramshaw's navigator, Flying Officer Dowie, came home from a Japanese prison camp and told how the Hudson had been shot into the sea as the pilot made his final bomb run. All on board except Dowie had been killed.

Five minutes later, Flight Lieutenant O'Brien returned for his second attack of the night. He noticed that the enemy transports were now anchored very close inshore and dropped his bombs squarely on one of them, his gunner observing what appeared to be two direct hits. All through O'Brien's attack, his aircraft had to run the gauntlet of intense and very accurate fire from the Japanese cruiser that was supporting the enemy landing, but although the aircraft sustained considerable damage its pilot nursed it back to base.

The fury went on hour after hour, the Australian crews taking off to make fresh attacks as soon as their aircraft were made ready by the toiling ground crews. The aircraft were operating from a single strip which, after weeks of almost continual rain, would normally have been classed unserviceable; amazingly, there were no accidents on take-off or landing.

Nevertheless, the battle was taking its toll. Two Hudsons had been shot down, and others returned in a progressively worse state after every sortie. The ground crews worked valiantly to patch them up with whatever materials they could find, but spares were in short supply and in the end two of the more severely damaged bombers were 'cannibalised' to keep the others flying.

Meanwhile, the Japanese infantry had begun landing on the beaches near Kota Bharu at 0300 hours. Seven thousand miles away, in mid-Pacific, American servicemen were either asleep or wending their way back to barracks from Oahu's bars and night-spots. There was still an hour and a quarter to go before the peace of an Hawaiian Sunday morning would be shattered by the bombs of Vice-Admiral Nagumo's carrier aircraft.

The Japanese at Kota Bharu were met by heavy rifle, machine-gun and mortar fire from defensive positions along the beach, manned mostly by Indian troops, and suffered appalling casualties. Nevertheless, the enemy quickly succeeded in breaking through the defences at several points, pushing into the screen of forest that separated Kota Bharu airfield from the beach.

On the airfield itself, Wing Commander Davis had no idea of how far the enemy landings had succeeded. Communications with the Army had broken down, and confusion was everywhere. Then, shortly after 0400 hours, ground crews working on the squadron's Hudsons reported that they were coming under fire from rifles and automatic weapons. The Japanese had reached the airfield perimeter.

Despite the added danger, the pace of work never slackened as the surviving Hudsons were refuelled and rearmed one after another. By this time, two of the enemy transports were burning fiercely, and shortly afterwards one of them blew up. She was the 9,749-ton *Awigasan Maru*, and the casualties among the troops still waiting to disembark were fearsome; some accounts later told how 5,000 Japanese died on this one ship alone.

The Australian aircrews now turned their attention to the enemy landing barges, bombing them and strafing the soldiers who were struggling ashore through the surf. It was later confirmed that the aircraft had destroyed at least twenty-four landing craft.

Dawn came, and as its grey light spread across the sea the aircrews began to have a real indication of the havoc their mast-height attacks had wrought during the night. A great pall of smoke rose up to meet the clouds from the shattered wrecks of the two freighters, while the shallows along the whole length of the beach were coloured pink with the blood of Japanese soldiers. The entire shoreline was thick with lifeless corpses, bobbing like driftwood on the tide.

At about 0800 hours, the hard-pressed crews of No. 1 Squadron received additional support when No. 8 Squadron RAAF, which had moved up to its war station at Kuantan, 150 miles down the coast, sent its Hudsons into action against the Japanese at Kota Bharu. During the first days of December this squadron had received six brand-new Bristol Beaufort torpedo bombers, but they were unarmed and their crews had received no operational training, so five of them had been ordered back to Australia straight away.

The sixth, still without any armament, was now flown up to Kota Bharu to carry out a reconnaissance mission over southern Thailand. It staggered back almost shot to ribbons after being attacked by enemy fighters, but its crew confirmed that the main Japanese convoy was off Singora and that about sixty Japanese fighters were based on the adjacent airfield.

This was bad news, for Singora was just over a hundred

miles away – easily within the combat radius of Japanese fighters. It was not long before they made their presence felt. At about 0900 hours, a flight of four Mitsubishi Zero fighters appeared over Kota Bharu and made several firing passes before disappearing to the north; fortunately they caused little damage, but air attacks continued sporadically throughout the morning and made air operations increasingly hazardous.

Sniper fire from the airfield perimeter also continued to be a nuisance, and although the Japanese were being held their bullets took an inevitable toll. To bolster the defensive firepower, the Australians removed machine guns from unserviceable Hudsons and mounted them on makeshift tripods. Apart from exchanging bursts of fire with the enemy on the perimeter, these weapons were also used as anti-aircraft guns in the hope that they might discourage at least some of the low-flying Japanese fighters. In this, they failed.

The battle of the barges went on, the Hudsons now attacking enemy craft on the Kelantan river. At 1100 hours the crews reported that the Japanese warships which had supported the invasion appeared to be withdrawing; if a strong force of Allied troops had been available to go into action at this point against the Japanese, the latter would probably have been wiped out. But no such force existed.

By midday on 8 December, No. 1 Squadron had only five airworthy Hudsons left out of its original thirteen. Desperate hand-to-hand fighting was now going on in the airfield's domestic site between the Japanese and a dwindling band of gallant Indian troops, and enemy snipers had now moved up to within 200 yards of where the ground crews were working on the surviving aircraft. The airmen sheltered as best they could behind wrecked aircraft and got on with their task, but there was no real cover and at 1400 hours Wing Commander Davis decided that the airfield would have to be evacuated.

Air and ground crews had now been operating non-stop in appalling conditions for nearly fourteen hours, and the men were exhausted. They would not know the facts until much later, but their efforts had come close to turning the Japanese invasion at Kota Bharu into a disaster. The air attacks, coupled with the gallant defence on the ground, had inflicted a staggering 15,000 casualties on the enemy.

Now it was over – or rather, just beginning. At 1430, the five serviceable Hudsons, each carrying two crews and as many airmen and equipment as they could pack in, took off under fire and flew to Kuantan.

The remainder of the personnel left by road at 1815. One man who should have been with them was Flight Lieutenant Jack Douglas, whose Hudson had been badly shot up during an attack on the Japanese cruiser earlier in the day. The ground crews had not had time to repair it, and so Douglas had orders to destroy it.

But Douglas was an unusually determined man. The Hudson's hydraulics had been shot to bits and the wing flaps were dangling uselessly, but the pilot grabbed a handful of wire and tied them in the 'up' position while enemy bullets crackled around his ears. Jumping into the cockpit, he managed to get the engines started and began to taxi towards the runway with Japanese soldiers running after him and taking pot-shots. Pausing only to pick up nine airmen who had been setting fire to damaged aircraft, he opened the throttles and somehow got the bullet-riddled machine into the air. He made the trip to Kuantan with his undercarriage down and the Hudson threatening to shake itself apart, eventually making a safe landing in almost total darkness.

Meanwhile, events were about to unfold that would rock the British nation to its foundations. In the early 1920s, the British government had decided to build a strong naval base in the Far East in the hope of ensuring that an increasingly powerful Japan would be deterred from threatening important British political and economic interests in South East Asia, Australasia and India. The choice of Singapore was based on the backward-looking assumption that naval power would be the key; in other words, that a battle fleet based on Singapore would be sufficient to deter and if necessary repel attack.

In the two decades that followed, several strategic factors came to be appreciated. First, it was unlikely that a large naval force could in reality be spared from elsewhere and get there in time; secondly, an attack was more likely to come overland from the north than via sea-borne assault, which meant that the key to Singapore's defence lay in the defence of the Malayan approaches; and thirdly, any successful defence of Malaya and Singapore would be impossible without the presence of a substantial air force. All three factors were appreciated as early as 1937 by the military authorities on the spot, who were convinced that the best way for the Japanese to attack would be to use

Indo-China as the base for landings in south Siam and north-east Malaya and then advance south.

The British Admiralty's plan to reinforce the Indian Ocean theatre with warships drawn from the Mediterranean Fleet, leaving the French Navy to concentrate on the Mediterranean, was dislocated by the collapse of France in 1940. In August 1941, another Admiralty plan envisaged reinforcing the Far East with six capital ships, a modern aircraft carrier and supporting light forces by the spring of 1942; in the meantime, the best that could be done was to send out the new battleship *Prince of Wales*, supported by the old battlecruiser *Repulse* (she had been launched in 1916) and the aircraft carrier *Indomitable*, which was to provide the essential air component. Even this plan was disrupted when the *Indomitable* ran aground off Jamaica while she was working up there; it was another fortnight before she was ready to sail.

The *Prince of Wales*, meanwhile, flagship of Rear-Admiral Sir Tom Phillips, had sailed from the Clyde on 25 October accompanied by the destroyers *Electra* and *Express*, under orders to proceed to Singapore via Freetown, Simonstown and Ceylon, where they were joined on 28 November by the *Repulse* from the Atlantic and the destroyers *Encounter* and *Jupiter* from the Mediterranean. The force reached Singapore on 2 December.

The Admiralty had always been reluctant to concentrate its warships on Singapore, preferring to base them further back on Ceylon; the fact that they were there at all was at the insistence of Winston Churchill, whose view –

supported by the Foreign Office – was that their presence would be enough to deter the Japanese from taking aggressive action. There were justifiable fears, in view of the *Indomitable*'s absence, of the force's vulnerability to enemy air attack. The RAF's air defences on Singapore and the Malay peninsula were woefully weak: about eighty American-built Brewster Buffalo fighters equipped four squadrons, two RAAF, one RAF and one RNZAF. All four squadrons had been formed within the last eight months, many of their pilots were inexperienced, and their aircraft – heavy, underpowered and underarmed – were wholly outclassed by the Japanese fighters they would soon encounter.

Not long before Admiral Phillips took up his new command (he had been Vice-Chief of Naval Staff) a friend made a cautionary remark to him. 'Tom, you've never believed in air. Never get out from under the air umbrella; if you do, you'll be for it.' They were prophetic words, and the man who made them was Air Marshal Sir Arthur Harris, soon to be appointed AOC-in-C Bomber Command.

Anxiety over the exposed position of Phillips's ships led the Admiralty to urge him to take them away from Singapore, and on 5 December 1941 the *Repulse*, under Captain Tennant, sailed for Port Darwin in North Australia. The next day, however, a Japanese convoy was reported off Indo-China, and Tennant was ordered back to Singapore to rejoin the flagship. Only hours later came the news of the Japanese attack on the US Pacific Fleet at Pearl Harbor, with simultaneous amphibious assaults elsewhere, including Malaya and Siam. On the evening of 8 December Admiral Phillips took the *Prince of Wales, Repulse* and four destroyers, collectively known as Force Z, to attack the Japanese amphibious forces which had landed at Singora.

Early the next morning Singapore advised him that no fighter cover would be available and that strong Japanese bomber forces were reported to be assembling in Siam, and this, together with the knowledge that his warships had been sighted by enemy reconnaissance aircraft, persuaded Phillips to abandon his sortie at 2015 on 9 December, reversing course for Singapore. (In fact, Force Z had also been sighted by the submarine I-65, but the position it transmitted was inaccurate, and other enemy submarines failed to detect the ships at this time.)

Just before midnight, Phillips received a signal that the Japanese were landing at Kuantan and he turned towards the coast, intending to intercept this new invasion force. The report was false, but in the early hours of 10 December Force Z was sighted by the submarine I-58. Its captain, Lieutenant Commander Kitamura, made an unsuccessful torpedo attack, then shadowed the British ships for five and a half hours, sending regular position reports that enabled reconnaissance aircraft of the 22nd Naval Air Flotilla to sight them and maintain contact. Already airborne from airfields in Indo-China were twenty-seven bombers and sixty-one torpedo aircraft, the flotilla's attack element, flying steadily south. They passed to the east of Force Z and flew on for a considerable distance before turning, and at about 1100 they sighted the ships.

The air attacks were executed with great skill and co-ordination, the high-level bombers – Mitsubishi G4M1s – running in at 12,000 feet to distract the attention of the warships' AA gunners while the torpedo bombers, G3M2s, initiated their torpedo runs from different directions. Two torpedo hits were quickly registered on the *Prince of Wales*, severely damaging her propellers and steering gear and putting many of her AA guns out of action. For some time the *Repulse*, by skilful evasive action, managed to avoid the attackers; but there were too many aircraft, and eventually she was hit by four torpedoes. At 1233 she rolled over and sank, and fifty minutes later the same fate overtook the flagship, which had meanwhile sustained two more torpedo hits. The accompanying destroyers picked up 2,081 officers and men; 840 were lost, among them Admiral Phillips and Captain Leach of the *Prince of Wales*. Captain Tennant of the *Repulse* survived, having been literally pushed off the bridge by his officers at the last moment.

No one in Singapore could understand the failure of Admiral Phillips to break radio silence and call for help, even when he knew his vessels had been sighted by the enemy. It was only an hour and a half later, when the ships had been under air attack for three quarters of an hour, that a signal was sent to inform Singapore what was happening, and even then it was Captain Tennant – not Phillips – who sent it. Eleven Buffaloes of No. 453 Squadron RAAF were immediately despatched and arrived in the area ninety minutes later, long after the Japanese had departed.

In Singapore, the news of the sinking of the warships

was greeted with disbelief. Nevertheless, there were few who seriously thought that the Japanese, now advancing down the Malay peninsula, would get anywhere near the Johore Strait, separating Singapore island from the mainland. And as for the notion that Singapore itself might fall – well, that was ridiculous. Everyone knew that the fortress was impregnable.

One

Rangoon, Burma, 28 January 1942

Wing Commander Ken Armstrong flexed his cramped limbs, moved a safe distance away from his Hurricane fighter, and touched a match to his already filled pipe. He savoured the aromatic smoke for a moment before letting it trickle in a stream from the corner of his mouth. Most of the other pilots had also landed; only three were still in the circuit, preparing to make their landing approach.

It was hard to believe that all twenty Hurricanes had arrived without mishap, for the journey had been long and dangerous. It was a week since they had left Cairo; from there they had flown via Palestine, Iraq, down the Persian Gulf to Bahrain and then on to Karachi, and from there across India to Calcutta and finally down the length of Burma to Mingaladon, near Rangoon. Without long-range tanks they couldn't have done it; the tanks would now have to be removed and the airframes lightened as much as possible, so as to raise the rate of climb in Burma's hot and humid climate and give the Hurricanes a fighting chance in turning combat with the Japanese fighters they were likely to encounter.

The newly arrived Hurricanes were dispersed some distance apart, and Armstrong stood on his own for a few minutes, puffing his pipe and looking around, before two other pilots came up to join him. They were his two flight commanders, Lieutenant Commander 'Dickie' Baird, who was attached to the RAF from the Fleet Air Arm, and Flight Lieutenant Stanislaw Kalinski, who had fought with the Polish and French Air Forces before escaping to England and finding his way into the RAF.

"Well," said Baird, expertly mimicking the larger of the Laurel and Hardy comedy duo, "this is another fine mess you've gotten me into."

Armstrong had to admit that Mingaladon was not one of the more attractive places he had visited. "I fear you are right, Dickie," he responded, looking around. On the far side of the airstrip, partly hidden among some stunted trees, he could make out some aircraft: a few stubby little Brewster Buffaloes, presumably the survivors of 67 Squadron, RAF – the fighter unit originally responsible for the defence of the whole of Burma – and some P-40 Tomahawks, belonging to a squadron of the American Volunteer Group, sent down from China in the previous December to lend a hand.

"Speaking of messes, I wonder where the Mess building is?"

"I have a nasty feeling it's that pile of rubble over there," Kalinski said, pointing. "This place has really taken a hammering."

They had all seen the scars of filled-in bomb craters scattered over the airstrip as they came in to land. Small groups of men, mostly Chinese, were still wielding shovels at various points, so there must have been a recent visitation by the Japanese.

Two ancient trucks came lurching up, followed by a fuel bowser. The trucks disgorged a couple of dozen airmen, who immediately set about fuelling and arming the Hurricanes, which had not carried ammunition during the long flight to Mingaladon in order to save weight. A senior NCO, a flight sergeant, climbed down from the cab of one of the trucks and spoke briefly to one of the newly arrived pilots, who pointed Armstrong out to him.

The flight sergeant came over and saluted, introducing himself as Cairns. "Better get the aircraft ready for action as quickly as we can, sir," he said. "We're expecting a big raid today, and we don't want anyone caught on the ground."

Armstrong nodded. "Right. In the meantime, where can we get a drink and something to eat?"

The flight sergeant smiled. "Oh, the Salvation Army van will be along in a minute, sir. There'll be plenty of tea and wads to be going on with."

"The what?" Baird said, thinking he had misheard.

"The Salvation Army van," Armstrong grinned, repeating the flight sergeant's words. It came as no surprise to him. In the desert, he'd seen Salvation Army mobile canteens drive up to the front line, under fire, to dispense their wares to grateful troops.

Armstrong was surprised, though, to discover that this particular van was in the charge of two elderly ladies, who proceeded to dispense tea and sandwiches with such unruffled calm that they might have been on Brighton seafront. He learned that they were members of a Salvation Army mission in Rangoon, established about a year earlier. Both of them had been in the colonial service for years.

"We quite like it in Rangoon," one of the women told Armstrong, as she dispensed tea from a large urn. "A lot of people don't, though; they say it's too drab, that even the Burmese hate it. It has a population of about half a million, and it's made up of an astonishing conglomeration of different peoples. We find it all very fascinating. The only trouble is, they don't seem to understand one another. I don't think they even try."

She handed Armstrong a mug of tea. He closed his eyes in bliss as he took a sip.

"I felt so sorry for them when the bombing started," the woman continued, suddenly conscious that she had an audience eager for news of the real situation in the Burmese capital. "The Japanese had been bombarding them with propaganda over the radio for weeks, and they were already confused when the first air raid came just before Christmas. That was terrible. There were no real air raid shelters, you know; just a few hurriedly from clay bricks, standing on the pavements. Nobody used them; the cement wasn't even dry."

Several of the other pilots, clutching their mugs of tea and wads of sandwiches, were now listening with interest to what the Salvation Army woman had to say.

"Well over a thousand people were killed in that first raid," she went on. "It started a mass exodus from the city. Bewildered, shocked labourers simply abandoned the docks, leaving scores of ships still loaded with war materials. Sanitary services broke down. Servants fled from hotels, private houses and boarding houses. Bus and tram drivers just vanished. The road north, the one leading to Prome, was packed with refugees. The poorer people carried all their possessions with them, on their heads, on push-carts or in rickshaws. The better off, of course, set off in their motor cars, well stocked with food, clothing and bedding. I noticed that many of the women looked worried, and it was because they were fearful of losing the boxes of jewels and money they had with them."

Armstrong shook his head slowly and rubbed the warm bowl of his pipe against his cheek.

"I hadn't realised it was as bad as that," he said. "We heard on the news, as we came through India, that Mr Churchill was full of praise for the people of Rangoon for standing by their posts. Sounds as though the reports he's been getting were a bit wide of the mark."

"Very," the woman said primly. "I'll never forget Rangoon, last Christmas. Dead bodies were left lying on the streets for days on end, covered by bits of sacking. There were piles of rotting garbage everywhere. Clouds of crows, too, and rats." She gave a little shudder.

Her companion, a few years younger, who up to now hadn't uttered a word, suddenly spoke up. "The bombers came back on Christmas Day, but by then there weren't many people left in the city. Why on earth the Governor didn't declare martial law, I can't imagine. The Americans were terribly critical. There's an American Military Mission in Rangoon, supervising this end of the Burma Road, and when more ships arrived, carrying cargoes of American war material for China, there was no labour to unload them. Why, if it hadn't been for Mr McLean-Brown, heaven knows what we should all have done."

Armstrong raised a questioning eyebrow. The elder of the two ladies smiled.

"A very blunt Yorkshireman," she explained, "who works for the Rangoon Docks Commission. He wanted to clean up the mess at Brooking Street Wharves, which had been heavily bombed. He rounded up all the Indian labourers he could find, told them that they would be taken by launch to the wharves, and that he would stay and work alongside them until the job was done. The workers were nervous, but agreed to go along with him provided the job could be finished by one o'clock in the afternoon, which is the time the Japanese bombers usually come over. They agreed to go back later, at the end of the danger period."

Armstrong glanced at his watch. It was eleven. He hoped the Japs were not going to be early today. "Please go on," he prompted. "I'd like as much background information as possible."

"Well," the Salvation Army woman continued, "off they went, and when they arrived at the wharves they found thousands of packets of cigarettes, all abandoned. Mr McLean-Brown told his workers they might help themselves to all they could carry, if they finished the job quickly. They did. He's a lovely man, and he has a young wife called Mara, and two little babies. They live in a bungalow beside the Rangoon river. Mara is just as determined as her husband. Their bungalow is surrounded by stacks of oil in drums, thousands of gallons of it, but she won't move to a safer place. If she did, it would mean that her husband wouldn't be able to get home, as he has no transport of his own. He starts very early and finishes late, you see."

They talked for some minutes longer, taking advantage of the lull while the Hurricanes were being refuelled and armed, and by the time the van trundled away Armstrong had formed a necessarily fragmented picture of the almost total chaos that reigned in Rangoon. But he had also learned that there were others of McLean-Brown's calibre – men like an anonymous Anglo-Indian, a waiter in the Strand Hotel, who had simply taken charge during the Christmas Day raid and restored order when the guests panicked. He was a waiter, and a couple of days later those same guests were once again treating him with their usual brand of mild condescension. After the second bombing raid only the manager, the assistant manager and the chef – all three Swiss – two Anglo-Indians and two Indian scullery hands were left. The chef continued to cook, and everyone lent a hand with the serving until there was no food left. Then the Strand Hotel, Rangoon's best, closed down for good.

And there were other Anglo-Indians and Indians who stayed put in the telegraph office after their superiors had fled. They stayed at their posts for a week, keeping the lines open until their equipment was destroyed. Much of the confusion, Armstrong discovered, was caused by the banks, which closed for eight days over the Christmas period at just the time when people wanted to draw money. And the scandal of the shipping, lying on the river fully laden with desperately needed war materials, became so acute that the editor of the Rangoon Gazette, a man called Stone, defied every Government-imposed reporting restriction to attack the bureaucrats on his front page. Under the headline 'FAITH IN OUR FIGHTING MEN: BUT SAVE US FROM NON-BELLIGERENT DOPES', he said in an article that shocked Rangoon officialdom:

There is little doubt that there are ships in Rangoon, and coming to Rangoon, loaded with goods, both for civil and military uses. The difficulty, apparently, is to get them unloaded, and as the Government fights shy of the excellent suggestion for labour battalions (although we cannot think why) we support the suggestion. Let us cut yards and yards of red tape, wound around the customs and port officials, and get down to essentials. The goods are here, and they have got to be unloaded, so let us get down to it and hang the cost. After all, there is a war on.

That was an indisputable fact which, somehow, seemed to have escaped the civilian administration in Rangoon.

Flight Sergeant Cairns came up and reported that the Hurricanes were refuelled and re-armed.

"Good," Armstrong said. "Now, where's flying control? There must be one – they talked to us on the way in."

Cairns pointed. "It's that brown tent over on the far side,

sir," he said. "The one with the sandbags around it. Jump into the truck, sir, and I'll give you a lift over."

Armstrong nodded. "Thanks, Flight. Dickie, come with me. Stan, keep an eye on things here, will you? I'll be back as soon as possible, as soon as I've found out what's what."

Leaving the Polish flight commander in temporary charge, Armstrong and Baird climbed into the truck's cab alongside the flight sergeant. A few minutes later they arrived at the flying control tent, identifiable now by the radio mast erected alongside. The sides of the tent had been rolled up to admit as much air as possible. There was one occupant, a youthful fair-haired man dressed in civilian slacks and an open-necked shirt, sitting at a trestle table on which a radio set was perched. A microphone was slung round his neck, and he was wearing headphones. He looked up as Armstrong's shadow fell across him, seemed puzzled for a moment, then removed his headset from one ear and stood up, grinning. He stuck out his hand.

"Hi," he said, "you're the new arrivals, I guess." The accent was unmistakably American. "The name's Glew. 'Sticky' to my pals. Kind of predictable, wouldn't you say?"

"Looks as though you've had a busy time," Armstrong said, shaking Glew's hand and introducing Baird. "Er – do you have some sort of rank?"

"Mister," Glew said, tapping the side of his nose with his index finger. "We're all misters here. Just call me Sticky. I'll call you sir, if you like," he added, glancing at the rank braid on the epaulettes of Armstrong's shirt. "You're a kind of colonel, aren't you?"

"Wing Commander," Armstrong informed him. "That's a kind of lootenant colonel. Name's Ken. And this lootenant commander, Royal Navy, is Dickie."

Glew grinned at Armstrong's deliberate American pronunciation. "Well, we're pretty informal around here," he said, "except in the air, where things become very professional. You'll see what I mean when you get to meet the guys. The Volunteer Group pilots, I mean."

"Where are they, incidentally?" Armstrong asked. We spotted one of two P-40s tucked away among the trees, but no sign of life."

"They're deployed to the forward airstrip at Moulmein," Glew told him. "There's a detachment of our troops holding on at Tenasserim, and our guys are providing all possible air support. I don't think they'll be there for long, though. Moulmein has been under heavy attack since the Japs crossed the Siamese border a week ago. Here, let me show you."

The American turned to a map board that was balanced on a blackboard easel next to his table, within easy reach. Various symbols had been drawn on the map in coloured crayon.

"All my own work," Glew said. "I like to keep up to date. Makes life a lot easier. Look, this is Tenasserim, this long thin tail here, running alongside the Siamese border for four hundred miles. It's only forty miles wide. Now, this is the way the Japs are coming." His finger slashed a line across Tenasserim and halted just short of Moulmein airfield, which stood near the coast on the Gulf of Martaban. "There are two Japanese divisions concentrated in this area," the American explained, "the thirty-third and fifty-fifth," as far as we know. We've only got small and scattered garrisons in Tenasserim, and between you and me they haven't a hope in hell of holding on for more than a couple more days. They'll have to be evacuated, most likely by sea. Then the Japs will come round the top end of the Gulf, here, cross the Sittang river and advance on Rangoon from the north-east. Or so I reckon."

It was, Armstrong decided, a very gloomy picture. He asked what sort of alert system was in place to give warning of approaching enemy aircraft. Glew gave a grimace.

"Pretty well non-existent," he told the RAF officer. "It's the layout of the Burma airfields that's the main problem." He indicated the map again. "See here. They're almost all sited on this long north-south line facing the Siamese frontier, running from Victoria Point in the far south through Mergui, Moulmein, Mingaladon, Toungoo, Heho and Namsang to Lashio up here in the north, a stone's throw from the Chinese border." His finger leap-frogged across the map as he spoke. "It's a goddam shame," he went on. "They're pretty good all-weather airfields, and the Burma Public Works Department did a fine job in building them. Trouble is, the Government told them to put them in the wrong place. They should have been built in the Irrawaddy Valley. As it is, there's just not enough warning time. We have to rely on the Burma Observer Corps, which was only formed a few weeks ago. But they have no wireless sets. That's their only means of communication." He pointed to a telephone that stood on the table beside the radio transceiver.

Armstrong sighed and turned to Baird, who was leafing through a series of sketches that had been stapled together. The drawings, Glew explained, had been made by a Volunteer Group pilot who had considerable artistic talent. They depicted various Japanese aircraft encountered in the fighting so far. The main fighter type, it seemed, was a snub-nosed monoplane with a radial engine and an enclosed cockpit, designed by the Japanese firm Nakajima. It also had a fixed undercarriage.

"Don't be fooled by that," Glew warned. "It's light and very manoeuvrable, and it can cause problems in a turning fight. But it tends to fall to bits if it takes a good solid hit, and it doesn't have self-sealing fuel tanks, so it burns well. So do their bombers. The Japanese Army Air Force uses the Type Ninety-Seven, built by Mitsubishi. We've knocked a lot of 'em down."

Armstrong wanted to know what had happened to the squadron of RAF Buffalo fighters.

"What's left of 'em have been pulled out to Magwe, up north," Glew explained. "The aircraft still here have been cannibalised for spare parts. The RAF have been having terrible trouble with spares, far worse than us."

The thought struck Armstrong that spare parts for the Hurricanes were supposed to have been shipped to Rangoon. He'd have to check on that urgently, he told himself, and made a note to ask Flight Sergeant Cairns if he knew anything about it.

"We'd better be getting back to our aircraft," he said, "since we seem to be Rangoon's sole air defence for the time being. Do we stay on the same frequency?"

Glew nodded. "Yes. If I hear anything, I'll put up a white flare, and give you your instructions once you're airborne. You'll have ten to fifteen minutes warning time, maximum. I hope it'll be enough."

"So do I," Armstrong agreed fervently. "Still, they might not come today, after all."

"Oh, they will," Glew said mildly. "They always do."

Two

Lieutenant Jiro Tanaka, Flight Commander with the 3rd Air Division of the Japanese Army Air Force, reached down and touched the hilt of the Samurai sword that rested beside his pilot's seat. It brought him reassurance, and renewed his courage, although Tanaka was not afraid of death. His only fear was that, in a momentary lapse, he might disgrace himself in the eyes of his Emperor, and lose face in front of his crew.

There were seven of them, stationed at various points in the long cabin of the twin-engined Mitsubishi Ki-21 heavy bomber. In addition to his co-pilot, Warrant Officer Horikoshi, the aircraft carried a navigator-bombardier, radio operator and three gunners. They formed a good crew, and they had been together a long time – since 1939, to be precise, when Tanaka's squadron had been assigned to the fighting in Manchuria. The pitiful Chinese Air Force had quickly been brushed aside by the greatly superior Japanese fighters, leaving the bombers free to roam at will, razing one Chinese city after another.

Now it was the turn of Burma to feel the weight of

Japanese bombs. In the past month Tanaka's squadron, operating from airfields in Siam, had flown twenty missions against Allied airfields in Burma and against Rangoon itself. Opposition in the air had been fierce, and several crews had not returned. Tanaka felt sad that the ashes of those men would never be sent home, to lie beside those of their ancestors.

Twenty-seven bombers were taking part in today's mission, against the enemy airfield of Mingaladon. They flew in three waves, each of nine aircraft formed up in arrowhead formation. They made a magnificent sight, Tanaka thought, with their dark green camouflage on which the *Hinomaru*, the red disk of the sun that rose from the sea, provided a splash of bright colour.

Tanaka was leading the second wave of bombers. Ahead of him, the first wave rose and fell gently on the currents of air that eddied up from the Dawn Range, the jungle-clad mountains that flanked the Thaungyin river. They were crossing the border now, and could expect trouble at any moment. Tanaka was thankful to catch an occasional glimpse of their fighter escort of Nakajima fighters, prowling watchfully overhead.

The attack came unexpectedly, from dead ahead, and it was over almost before the Japanese crews had time to register that it was happening. Half a dozen single-engined aircraft flashed through the of first wave of Ki-21s, diving hard, streamers of grey smoke curling from their wings as they opened fire. One of them passed underneath Tanaka's bomber and a gunner fired a burst at it, earning a sharp rebuke from the pilot.

"Wait until they are a direct threat to us, you dolt! Do not waste ammunition!"

The leading wave of Ki-21s flew steady on, apparently unscathed. Then the fighters came in again, this time from astern, diving at top speed to make their attack and then climbing away steeply. A gunner reported that more enemy fighters were engaging the Japanese fighter escort, up above.

They had all had a good look at the enemy fighters by this time. They were Curtiss P-40s, with a wicked-looking shark's mouth painted on each of their noses. Tanaka had never encountered them so close to the border before; they must be operating from a forward airfield, he told himself. Although the Curtiss fighters bore the markings of the Chinese Air Force, a twelve-pointed white star on a blue background, Tanaka knew that they were flown by Americans. This was going to be a tough fight, for the bombers were still a long way from their target.

A Japanese fighter dropped through the bomber formation, trailing a ribbon of flame. A couple of thousand feet lower down it exploded like a grenade, sending incandescent fragments showering into the jungle. There was no parachute, but Tanaka had not expected to see one. Japanese aircrew carried parachutes, but not one of them would have dreamed of bailing out except in an emergency over his own territory. To be captured by the enemy was unthinkable, the worst possible dishonour. If a man was unfortunate enough to survive a crash-landing in enemy territory, his duty was to kill as many of the enemy as possible, and then kill himself, either by *seppuku*

– the traditional stomach-cutting – or by any other means available.

The Japanese fighters outnumbered the enemy by five to one, and soon the Americans had to abandon their attacks on the bombers in order to concentrate on their own survival. They had, however, inflicted damage on the bombers. A Mitsubishi on the extreme left of the leading flight suddenly wavered and dropped out of formation, diving away in a long curve that only ended when it struck the jungle far below, its bomb load exploding in a soundless geyser of smoke. Tanaka had seen a P-40 make a beam attack on it, so the pilots and maybe other crew members must have been killed. There had been no sign of fire.

The pilots of two other bombers, too badly damaged to continue, reported that they were abandoning the mission and returning to base. There was no dishonour in that. To push on would have simply been an act of folly. As it was, if luck was on their side, they would live to fly and fight another day.

After flying due west for some time the Japanese formation came to the broad estuary of the Sittang river, where it altered course to the south-west, heading for Rangoon and its adjacent airfield. The Americans, Tanaka thought, had clearly made a serious mistake; by deploying their fighters close to the border with Siam, they had left their main base undefended. It was just as well, because the escort of Nakajima fighters, short of fuel after the battle with the Americans, reported that it could no longer continue to accompany the bombers.

Mingaladon was twenty miles ahead. On the orders of the squadron leader, Captain Watanabe, the three flights of bombers closed up into tighter formation. All the remaining twenty-four aircraft would release their bombs on his signal. Each aircraft was carrying 1,600 pounds of bombs, which meant that very shortly Mingaladon airfield would be blasted by over seventeen tons of high explosive, making it unusable for some time.

The formation cruised on serenely, passing between columns of white cloud that towered up for several thousands of feet on either side. Tanaka found himself whistling softly between his teeth; it was a habit of his, whenever growing excitement caused adrenalin to start coursing through his veins. He calculated that the bombers would be able to make their attack and be back across the border before the American fighters had time to refuel and re-arm for a second interception, so there would only be the anti-aircraft fire over Mingaladon to worry about, and that was so weak as to present a negligible threat. Nevertheless, he ordered his gunners to be on the alert.

It was just as well, for it was one of his gunners who was the first to see the approaching danger, coming up fast from underneath, on the right. Tanaka, in the left-hand pilot's seat, could not yet see the enemy fighters, but his co-pilot, Horikoshi, kept up a running commentary as he peered down through the glazed panels on his side of the cockpit.

"Four, five, six, seven . . . Turning now, sir, still climbing. Level with the formation now, turning to get up-sun.

Single-engined monoplanes. Not P-40s. I apologise most humbly, sir, but I am unable to identify them."

The bomber crews astern of them were calling out warnings of more fighters, apparently coming in from all directions. Suddenly, Tanaka's gunners opened fire, the recoil of their guns making the aircraft tremble. A shadow flitted over the top of the bomber's cockpit, and for an instant, before the enemy fighter vanished, Tanaka had a vivid impression of a strange, sandy camouflage scheme with roundels stamped on it. He had seen those roundels before, on the rotund Brewster Buffaloes that had confronted the Japanese bombers in their earlier attacks on Rangoon. Whatever these fighters were, they were British; he was now in no doubt about that.

The sandy camouflage puzzled him. He had no way of knowing that the fighters had been in North Africa just a couple of weeks earlier.

Another of the strange fighters attached itself to the tail of Captain Watanabe's bomber. The intermittent smoke trails that whipped back from its wings indicated that the pilot was firing in short bursts, and he was firing from very close range. A professional, Tanaka thought. A man who knows what he's about.

An instant later, the enemy fighter sheered away as the bomber burst into flames. It was finished, the flames bursting from its unsealed fuel tanks and spreading from wingtip to wingtip with terrifying speed. Its nose went down and the blazing mass disappeared under Tanaka's aircraft as he flew through the stinking oily smoke that marked its final plunge.

Over the radio, Watanabe gave a last, defiant scream as he prepared to meet the gods of his ancestors.

"Banzai! Tenno-heika banzai!" Ten thousand years to the Emperor!

Tanaka offered up a brief prayer for the soul of his squadron commander. He was now in charge of the mission, and he now instructed the pilots of the seven surviving bombers of the leading flight to close their ranks and maintain their course. They would now bomb on his orders.

He had scarcely issued his instructions when his own bomber shuddered as it took hits, the enemy's bullets sounding like hailstones on its metal fuselage. Out of his cockpit window, he saw rents appear in the fabric-covered port aileron. Then the pounding stopped.

"Gunners, report!" he ordered sharply. They told him that the bomber had come under attack from two fighters, but that they had been beaten off.

"Target in two minutes, sir," his bombardier told him calmly. Tanaka could already see it, a patch of light brown earth surrounded by green.

The enemy fighters were still harassing the formation. Two more bombers were already falling in flames. One of his gunners reported that he had seen a fighter go down, and that the pilot had baled out.

The leading flight was suddenly subjected to a savage attack from head on by three fighters, which broke off at the last moment and dived away beneath, pursued by futile bursts of fire from the following bombers. One of the aircraft in the leading formation suddenly reared up like a stricken horse, pulled violently to one side and collided with the next bomber in line. A vast orange and black explosion filled the sky as two bomb loads detonated simultaneously. The second wave of bombers flew on through the expanding smoke cloud, from which fell an incandescent mass of tangled debris.

The fighters now seemed to be concentrating on the rearmost flight, which reported two bombers destroyed in the space of thirty seconds. Twenty bombers now remained out of the original formation of twenty-nine, and still the fighters kept on coming in.

It was impossible to maintain formation in the face of such determined attacks. The few surviving bombers of the leading flight were already becoming scattered, despite Tanaka's exhortations to their pilots, whose nerve seemed to have suffered after Watanabe's death. One of them suddenly jettisoned his bomb load, in defiance of Tanaka's orders, and turned away. The others continued on, more afraid of Tanaka than the enemy.

"Let him pray that he is shot down on the way home," Tanaka snarled to himself, grinding his teeth.

"Bombing in thirty seconds, sir," the bombardier said, peering down from his position in the nose. "Turn left three degrees."

There was a creaking sound as the man opened the bomb doors, and the Ki-21 buffeted with the sudden drag.

Tanaka moved the control column, which felt sluggish because of the bullet-torn aileron. He tried to relax, yet at the same time retain firm control, feeling every movement of the aircraft through his sensitive hands.

"Ten seconds, sir," the bombardier said.

"Very well." He pressed the button to transmit over the radio. "Bombing in five seconds . . . four . . . three . . . two . . . one . . . release!"

The Ki-21 jumped as its bomb load fell away. Ahead of him, the surviving aircraft of the leading flight dropped their bombs in unison and then steep-turned away from the target in a well-practised manoeuvre, each bomber following its neighbour. The two other flights followed suit.

"Form up in flights of five, line astern, and keep close," Tanaka ordered as the bombers turned on to a south-easterly course. "Rear gunner, report."

"Sir, I humbly beg to report that the target area is obscured by smoke," the man replied. The pilot grunted with satisfaction. Later on, a high-flying reconnaissance aircraft would be sent over to photograph the damage.

The bombers, maintaining tight formation in four boxes of five, flew on towards their base at 13,000 feet. Many of them had sustained battle damage; it was likely to be several days before they could mount another raid in strength.

At Mingaladon, the Hurricane pilots landed as best they could, weaving between the new bomb craters as they taxied to their dispersals. Two of the fighters were missing, and one of the pilots had been seen to bale out. A Burma Police patrol was sent out to look for him. They brought him in the next morning, shaken but otherwise unhurt.

Armstrong and his pilots, jubilant at their success, were told that they were to be quartered at the Mingaladon Golf Club, just outside Rangoon. It was early in the evening when they arrived, the management and few guests looking on with expressions that were a mixture of horror and incredulity as eighteen young men, tired, sweaty and clutching odds and ends of kit, trooped into the foyer. A suave under-manager came up to Armstrong and took him conspiratorially by the elbow.

"Sir," he said, "we were told only that we were to accommodate the officers. Nothing was said about non-commissioned officers. Other ranks are not allowed in the Club, I'm afraid."

"They are now," Armstrong told him bluntly. "They're hungry, thirsty and weary, and they risked their necks today. Now, I want drinks for them, I want meals for them, and then I want beds for them, in that order."

"But, sir . . ."

"Either that, or we set fire to your bloody club," Armstrong whispered in his ear. "Now, where's the bar?"

The bar proved to be surprisingly well stocked, and the Indian bartender, clearly delighted by the discomfort of the resident *burra sahibs*, set about serving drinks with a will.

Dickie Baird raised a glass of gin and tonic to his lips, looked around at the clientele in their dinner jackets and evening gowns, and shook his head in amazement. "Just take a look at that lot," he said. "You wouldn't think the Japs were a few miles down the road."

"It was the same in Singapore."

The speaker was a tall man dressed in khaki slacks and a dark green bush shirt, who was leaning with both elbows resting on the bar counter. They hadn't really taken any notice of him until now, having assumed him to be a club member. He had receding hair and might have been anywhere between twenty-five and forty. He spoke with a slight Australian accent. He straightened up, turned to face them and stuck out a hand.

"Good to see you blokes. I'm Bill Donahue, war correspondent. I came to interview the Americans, but they don't seem to be here. I saw your scrap this afternoon, though. Some show, that. Well done. They say a Jap bomber crashed a few miles east of here. Wouldn't mind taking a look at that in the morning."

"You've come from Singapore?" Armstrong queried.

Donahue nodded."Yeah. Came over in a Catalina, just before daybreak. There are three of us, as a matter of fact. The others have still got their heads down. Slept through all the action earlier on."

He took a pull at his beer and made a face. "Bloody repulsive, but it's all they've got, and I don't drink spirits. Not yet, anyway." He nodded towards the diners. "If you think this is all pretty snobbish, you should have seen the clubs in Singapore. I never went to the Bengal Club, which I gather is the most exclusive club in the Orient, but I was taken to the Singapore Club, where all the top businessmen meet. The locals call 'em *Tuans Besar*, which roughly translates as big shots. I went for lunch there one day – it was in October, not long after I arrived – and I'd never seen so much food. There must have been two dozen different courses to choose from. It was a bit different when I went up to Khota Baru to visit the Australian squadron a couple of weeks later, I can tell you."

A shrill cry that sounded like *tauk-teh* made them all jump. It was repeated several times, and seemed to come from somewhere in the rafters. The diners took no notice and went on eating.

"What the devil was that?" Eamonn O'Day queried, peering up into the shadows.

"Is lizard, sir," the smiling Indian steward informed him. "*Tauk-teh*. Bring good or bad luck. When he call eight times, is good luck for the house and all persons in it."

"How many times did he call just now?"

"Six, sir. Not so good."

"Oh, hell," the Irish flight lieutenant said. "We'd better have another drink."

"You were saying about Khota Baru," Armstrong prompted. Donahue cleared his throat.

"Oh, yes. A very different story. Apart from the fact that the whole damn place was awash with water, the food was the worst I've every tasted. Boiled potatoes swimming around in a thin stew, with a bit of bread and jam to finish off. There was a shortage of drinking water, too, and what there was had to be heavily chlorinated. Everybody on the station had bad guts, and I don't wonder. I was glad to get away." His eyes took on a faraway look.

"Poor beggars, they fought until they had nothing left to fight with when the Japs invaded. All while those fat bastards in Singapore were stuffing their faces and doing precisely nothing to help . . ."

"You must have been in Singapore when the *Prince of Wales* and *Repulse* were sunk," Dickie Baird said quietly. There was a pause of several seconds, then Donahue said:

"Not exactly. You see, I was actually on the *Repulse*, together with a couple of other correspondents and a photographer or two. We were supposed to be on the *Prince of Wales*, but the captain, or admiral, or whatever, said there wasn't room for us and flatly refused to have us on board."

He stared intently at Baird. "Don't believe what anyone tells you about the Japs," he said. "Everyone thought that we'd be subjected to reckless air attacks by individual aircraft coming in from all angles. We thought they'd be like flying suicide squads, intent on putting their bombs and torpedoes into us even if it meant diving into us. In fact, it wasn't like that at all."

He turned to the barman and ordered another beer before continuing.

"Some of the chaps, who'd seen the German and Italian air forces in action, said they'd never seen flying like it. They came at us in formation, even the torpedo-bombers, and they simply ignored our anti-aircraft fire. It was beautiful discipline, and it worked. Well, I daresay you know the rest. I was picked up by the Australian destroyer *Vampire*, half poisoned by fuel oil. That's not an experience I wish to repeat, I'll tell you. I stank of the stuff for a fortnight."

He picked up his refilled beer glass, half raised it to his mouth and then replaced the drink untouched on the bar.

"I'll tell you something else the Japs are very good at," he went on, "and that's propaganda. Not only did they drop bombs on Malaya and Singapore; they also dropped leaflets by the thousand, in every language spoken in

44

the peninsula. Mind you, some of their content was a bit naïve. I remember one, purporting to be a facsimile of a newspaper special edition, which declared that the United States had opened up separate peace negotiations with Japan. Another, addressed to the officers and men of the British Army, had quite a remarkable turn of phrase. I recall it word for word. 'Why,' it asked, 'do you submit to the intolerable torture of malarial mosquitoes merely to pamper the British aristocrat? Do not dedicate your lives merely to fatten the British high-hat.' It made us chuckle, until we realised that, as execrable as the English was, none of us knew a single European who could even have made a stab at speaking or writing Japanese – if you get my point.

"There were lots of other themes, most of them quite crude. One leaflet, addressed to Indian troops, showed a British officer cowering in the rear while the Indians fought the enemy. Another contained a crude drawing of a fat white man with a whiskey glass in his hand, treading a Malay underfoot. Yet another, aimed at the Australian troops, showed a naked blonde tart draped over a bed, wailing 'Oh, Johnny, come back to me. I am so lonely without you!' She got a lot of backsides wiped on her."

Donahue's face became suddenly serious. "There were some leaflets that caused a lot of bother, though. One was dropped on Singapore and advised the population to get out of the city on a certain date. A lot of the natives did, and the essential services suffered badly as a result. Nothing happened on that day, of course. But the leaflet that did stir up the troops was a copy of a letter taken from the body of dead Australian. It was from his wife, giving news of home, his kids and so on. A real bastard, that one."

Donahue picked up his glass again and this time drained it in one long swallow. "I'm whacked," he told them. "I'm off to bed. See you blokes around."

Baird surveyed the journalist's retreating back and shook his head slowly. "Quite a chap," he remarked to no one in particular. "We're here because the Air Force tells us we have to be. He doesn't. Takes all sorts, I suppose."

They had a mediocre meal of fish and vegetables, welcome nonetheless, and went off to seek their billets. They were to be accommodated in some long wooden huts some distance from the Golf Club; the huts had been divided into small rooms that were little more than cubby-holes. Armstrong never discovered why they had been built.

On the way, a few of the pilots started to sing, their spirits lifted by a few drinks and the food. As they passed a wooden bungalow, they were hailed from the darkness by a petulant English voice.

"I say, you chaps, would you mind making just a little less noise? You sound like a bunch of ruffians. It's just not on, you know. If it happens again, I shall have to inform the committee. This is a quiet country club. I know there's a war on, but it's no excuse for ungentlemanly behaviour."

"I say," someone called out in response, "do you actually mean 'Welcome to Burma, brave defenders of my wife's honour?'"

"Take up the white man's burden," someone else said

on a loud voice, quoting Rudyard Kipling. "Send forth the best ye breed . . ."

"Bollocks!" they chorused in unison.

From the shadows of the bungalow, there was silence.

Three

Mingaladon, 31 January 1942

The P-40s of the American Volunteer Group returned to Mingaladon soon after dawn, their Allison engines whistling and crackling as they touched down in pairs and taxied to their dispersals. There were fifteen of them out of the original eighteen that had set out for Moulmein; one had been lost in combat, and two more destroyed on the ground in a strafing attack by Japanese fighters. On the credit side, they had claimed a dozen enemy aircraft shot down during their short deployment close to the Siamese border.

The AVG's 1st Pursuit Squadron was led by Squadron Leader Bob Sandell. Armstrong took to him immediately; in fact, all the RAF pilots and their American counterparts quickly slipped into easy friendships born of their mutual professionalism.

Sandell told Armstrong how, during their stay at Moulmein, the AVG had decided to carry the war to the enemy. Moulmein was just within range of the Japanese airfield of Raheng, in Siam, and six P-40s, under the command of Squadron Leader Jack Newkirk, had carried out a strafing attack on the Japanese base. Two enemy fighters were in the circuit when the Americans arrived overhead like thunderbolts; both were shot down before their pilots had a chance to take evasive action. Leaving four P-40s as top cover, Newkirk and his wingman, David L. 'Tex' Hill, dived on a line of parked enemy machines and raked them from end to end, leaving six of them in flames. Turning steeply, the P-40s came back again, howling across the field at twenty feet and sending streams of bullets into the installations. Japanese soldiers fired at them fruitlessly with rifles. Then the Americans were gone, speeding back across the Burmese border.

Further attacks on Japanese airfields in Siam were mounted during January, but because of the range problem their damaging effect was strictly limited and they were more of a nuisance to the enemy than a serious threat. Then, on 20 January 1942, the whole situation underwent a dramatic change when Japanese forces crossed the border and advanced rapidly into southern Burma. Within days Moulmein itself was under heavy attack, and at dawn on the last day of the month a withdrawal was ordered, the Americans taking off under enemy shellfire.

As they drank coffee together in the flying control tent, Sandell told Armstrong in great detail about the origins of the American Volunteer Group. They went back to May 1937, when a retired United States Army Air Corps officer named Claire Chennault arrived in China at the request of General Chiang Kai-shek's government to carry out a survey of the Chinese Air Force. Chennault, whose controversial views on air defence had not endeared him to many colleagues in the USA, expected to remain in

China for only a few months. He had no inkling that he would still be there in December 1941, when the Japanese attacked Pearl Harbor.

Chennault was appalled by what he saw as he toured the Chinese Air Force's training schools during that summer of 1937. The quality of both pilots and aircraft was terrible. At Loyang, one of the principal flying schools, where the instructors were Italian, cadets graduated whether they could fly adequately or not.

The shortcomings became brutally apparent in July 1937, when Japanese forces invaded Manchuria and began pushing inland along the Yangtse river. Although the Chinese Air Force had five hundred aircraft, only ninety-one were airworthy and only a handful of pilots were fit to fly them in action. The first skirmishes with the highly trained Japanese showed not only that the Chinese Air Force had no means of slowing down the enemy advance, but that it was also totally incapable of defending China's cities against air attack. Within weeks, the Japanese had gained complete air superiority, and for the next three years they were to use north-east China as a virtual operational training area for their combat pilots. It was small wonder that the Japanese Army and Navy Air Forces, by December 1941, were tactically among the world's best.

By October 1937, following bitter fighting in the Shang-hai sector, the effective strength of the Chinese Air Force was twelve aircraft. In a desperate bid to save the situation an international air squadron was formed, composed of British, Dutch and American volunteers and armed with a motley collection of aircraft purchased by an American arms dealer. Although the squadron flew many missions during the winter of 1937-8, it was hopelessly outclassed and its operations came to an abrupt end early in 1938, when its base at Hankow was destroyed.

It was the Russians who brought the first real aid to the Chinese. Late in 1937, six Soviet Air Force squadrons – four of fighters and two of bombers – were sent to China, together with 350 personnel. The commander of the Russian contingent was Colonel Stefan Suprun, fresh from a tour of duty in the Spanish Civil War. Operating a mixture of I-15 and I-16 fighters, the Russians went into action early in 1938, fighting hard and continuously until early March, when they were withdrawn for a rest. Their place was taken by the first batch of Russian-trained Chinese pilots, who were flung into action in the defence of Nanking, but once again they proved no match for the Japanese and they were decimated.

Between 1938 and 1940, it was the Russians who provided the nucleus of China's air defences. Soviet air strength in China increased all the time, and when Japanese troops invaded Mongolian territory in the summer of 1939 they met the attack with 580 aircraft, including 350 fighters. The Japanese, on the other hand, had some 450 combat aircraft in China, and when the two sides clashed some of the biggest air battles seen since 1918 took place over the Khalkhin river, the disputed frontier territory.

At the same time, several Russian squadrons had exchanged their I-15s for the more modern I-153, with a retractable undercarriage, and the appearance of these aircraft over the Khalkhin took the Japanese fighter pilots completely by surprise. The Russians would approach the combat area with their undercarriages lowered, giving the impression that they were slower I-15s and inviting the Japanese to attack them. Once the enemy had committed themselves, the Russians would pull up their landing gear and neatly turn the tables.

Occasionally, the sky over the river was covered by a twisting mêlée of up to 200 aircraft as big formations clashed head on. The Japanese usually emerged the worse from these encounters; although their principal fighter type, the Nakajima Ki-27, could hold its own against the I-153, it was outclassed in speed and firepower by its most frequent opponent – the I-16, which the Japanese dubbed *Abu* (Gadfly). Although there was not a great deal of difference in terms of skill between Russian and Japanese pilots, Russian tactics were generally better as a consequence of combat lessons learned in Spain, where they had fought Spanish Nationalist, German and Italian pilots. The armament of their fighters was better, too; four 7.62mm machine guns carried by the I-16 compared with the twin 7.7mm weapons mounted in both the Ki-27 and the other main Japanese fighter, the Mitsubishi A5M. The I-153 also had four 7.62s, as well as provision for six RS-82 air-to-ground rockets under the wings. On several occasions over the Khalkhin, RS-82s were launched at Japanese fighters in the course of a dogfight.

The fighting between the Russians and the Japanese

petered out in the autumn of 1939. Japan had planned further offensives into Mongolia, but was persuaded to call off the idea by her ally, Germany, who – with the invasion of Poland in the offing – was anxious to maintain friendly relations with the Soviet Union. This left the Japanese free to step up their air attacks on targets in south-west China, and by the summer of 1940 the situation was once more critical.

Claire Chennault had now been in the country for three years, acting as an air adviser to Chiang Kai-shek and making a careful study of the tactics emerging from the fighting in the north. He now held the rank of colonel in the Chinese Air Force and worked in close conjunction with Mao Pang-tso, the CAF's Director of Operations. In October 1940, both men were summoned to a conference with Chiang, who proposed sending them on a mission to the United States to buy American fighters and hire the pilots to fly them.

Chennault's 'shopping list' envisaged the purchase of 660 aircraft, 500 of them combat types, enough materials to build 14 large airfields and 122 landing strips, plus sufficient ammunition and spares for a year's operational flying. Officials of the US Presidential Liaison Committee, which had to approve the purchase of arms for overseas countries in the United States, viewed the proposals with incredulity when Chennault and Mao presented them in November 1940. America's aviation industry was already working flat out to provide modern combat aircraft for the nation's own army and navy, as well as for Great Britain, and the Pentagon's military leaders were initially opposed to the idea of providing badly needed hardware for a remote conflict.

They had reckoned, however, without the determination of Claire Chennault. He spent the next few weeks drumming up support in the White House. He acquired a group of powerful backers, including Henry Morgenthau, Secretary to the Treasury, and in the end persuaded President Roosevelt himself to give his blessing to the scheme. With White House approval secured, Chennault and Mao began an extensive tour of aircraft factories throughout the United States, in search of suitable combat aircraft.

It was a far from easy task. The demands of the armed forces outstripped production, and the Royal Air Force had first priority among overseas customers. For a time, it looked as though Chennault would return to China empty handed. Then Burdette Wright, Vice-President of the Curtiss-Wright Corporation, and William D. Pawley – the arms agent who had supplied aircraft for the international air squadron – came to his rescue. Between them, they arranged for Chennault to purchase one hundred P-40B fighters. These had originally been offered to the RAF, but had been rejected on the grounds that they were not sufficiently advanced. The RAF finally settled for the improved P-40E version, which they called the Kittyhawk, and in January 1941 the P-40Bs were sold to the Chinese Government at a cost of nearly nine million dollars.

While the fighters were being crated for delivery, Chennault set about recruiting volunteers. The whole operation went ahead in strict secrecy, recruitment being carried out under cover by the Central Aircraft Manufacturing Company (CAMCO). Between April and July 1941, CAMCO agents toured American air bases in search of volunteers for the American Volunteer Group. They offered pilots a salary of between $600 and $750 per month, plus expenses, accommodation and thirty days' paid annual leave. Also – although this never appeared in the contract, for obvious reasons – pilots were promised a bonus of $500 for every Japanese aircraft they destroyed. Ground crews were offered salaries ranging from $150 to $350 per month, depending on their skills.

The volunteers, all of them serving US military personnel, were bound to CAMCO by a one-year contract. They would retain their American citizenship, and after their service in China they would return to their military units with no loss of seniority.

By the end of June 1941 CAMCO's agents had recruited a hundred pilots and a hundred and fifty mechanics. Not all of them were as experiences as Chennault would have wished, but finding volunteers had proved more difficult than he had expected and some compromise had been necessary.

The first contingent of volunteers arrived in Rangoon on 28 July and from there went to Kyedaw airfield, 170 miles further north. Chennault had originally planned to use Kunming in China as the AVG's main operational base, but this field was not completed in time and so Kyedaw had to be used as an alternative, with the tacit approval of the British War Office and the colonial administration in Burma. Conditions at Kyedaw were frightful, with tropical diseases such as malaria and dysentery rife in the hot, humid climate, and illness was a perpetual battle with which the Americans – some of whom had never been overseas before – had to contend.

The training programme was hard, too. For a start, not many of the volunteers were experienced fighter pilots, so they all had to start virtually from scratch. Then, to their astonishment, Chennault told them to forget the air fighting tactics they had been taught in the United States. Combat flying would be based on the 'pair', with the leading aircraft attacking and the number two guarding his tail. These tactics had been pioneered by the German air aces of the Great War, refined during combat in Spain, and were being used successfully in the European air war.

Day after day the AVG pilots flew and trained until Chennault's air fighting rules were second nature to them. Then, and only then, did they begin to study the enemy's tactics.

It was now that Chennault's careful study of Japanese airmen in action paid dividends. First of all, he hammered home the lesson that, far from being second-rate as portrayed in western circles, the Japanese were excellent, highly trained pilots whose air combat discipline was second to none. Their handling of large bomber formations was particularly good, so Chennault trained his men to break up such formations and destroy their cohesion. Marksmanship was of vital importance, and AVG pilots spent hours poring over drawings of the enemy bombers they were likely to encounter, picking out vulnerable spots such as the fuel tanks, which in most Japanese types were inadequately protected.

As far as combat with enemy fighters was concerned, Chennault stressed that the Nakajima and Mitsubishi types were more manoeuvrable than the P-40, so he taught his pilots to make use of the American fighter's heavier weight and higher speed by making fast diving attacks. A short, accurately placed burst from the P-40's six machine guns would usually be sufficient to cripple a less robust opponent.

Volunteer Group pilots spent some seventy-two hours working on these tactics in the classroom, followed by at least sixty hours' fighting practice in the air. They learned to cruise in pairs at maximum altitude and make high-speed passes at simulated enemy aircraft below, avoiding turning manoeuvres and fighting on the climb-and-dive. Inevitably, with spare parts in short supply, this arduous training took its toll of the P-40s; by the first week of December 1941, only fifty-five of the original hundred aircraft were serviceable.

Gradually, a formidable *esprit de corps* grew among the AVG personnel as their confidence increased. By December, Chennault had forged them into a highly efficient fighting unit, yet the pretence of being civilian employees under contract was still carefully fostered. There were no ranks as such. Pilots were designated by the position they held within the organisation, such as squadron leader, flight leader and wingman.

Soon after the Japanese attack on Pearl Harbor, it was decided to divide the resources of the AVG. Kyedaw airfield was abandoned, and on 10 December 1941 twenty-one P-40s flew to Mingaladon under the command of Squadron Leader Arrives Olson. The other thirty-four air-worthy machines, led by Squadron Leader Robert Sandell, flew north-east to the newly completed base at Kunming, close to China's lifeline: the vital Burma road.

It was Bob Sandell's 1st Pursuit Squadron which made first contact with the enemy. It happened on the morning of 20 December, when ten P-40s were scrambled to intercept a force of Japanese bombers heading for Kunming. The enemy had apparently not expected fighter opposition, for the ten twin-engined Mitsubishi Ki-21 bombers were unescorted. Sandell's pilots had a field day; six bombers went down in flames as the P-40s ripped into their forma-tion. Only one P-40 failed to return; its pilot, Ed Rector, successfully made a forced landing.

At Mingaladon, the men of Arivs Olson's 3rd Pursuit Squadron heard of this victory with envy and wondered when their turn would come. They did not have long to wait. On the twenty-third, the Japanese appeared over Rangoon in strength and the AVG took off to intercept them, accompanied by the RAF's Buffaloes. While the latter took on the escorting Ki-27 fighters, Olson's twelve P-40s dived on the bomber formation. The first AVG pilot to score was Ken Jernstedt, who chopped away at a Mitsubishi until it went down with both engines streaming flames. His colleague, Charles Older, fired at a second bomber and found himself flying through a cloud of smoke and debris as the enemy's bomb load exploded, scatter-ing wreckage across the sky. Fierce battles raged over

Rangoon as the American and British pilots pressed home their attacks. They destroyed six bombers and four fighters, but the RAF lost five Buffaloes and the Americans four P-40s. Two American pilots baled out and were saved, although one of them – Flight Leader Paul J. Greene – had some nasty moments when a Japanese fighter took a shot at him as he floated down under his parachute. Fortunately, the enemy pilot's aim was poor.

The Americans avenged their losses on Christmas Day, when the Japanese mounted a second major raid on Rangoon with sixty bombers escorted by twenty fighters. The enemy formation split up some distance away from the city, one half heading for Mingaladon airfield and the other for Rangoon's docks. This time, the Allied pilots had received plenty of warning of the attack, and while the RAF's Buffaloes provided top cover over Rangoon the AVG's thirteen P-40s made contact with the enemy ten miles away. The Americans had the advantage of height, and while one P-40 flight attacked the fighter escort – composed of Mitsubishi Zeros on this occasion – the rest tore into the bombers, using Chennault's tactics to good effect.

Within minutes, the impeccable Japanese formation had been torn to shreds, and the AVG's first three fighter aces had been created. Charles Older destroyed four bombers; Robert P. 'Duke' Hedman got four bombers and a Zero; and three bombers fell to the guns of Robert T. Smith. It was not a bad day's work for a retired acrobat, as Smith had fictitiously registered himself *en route* to Burma from the United States.

As the Japanese bombers scattered, the AVG pilots fell upon them, shooting one after another out of the sky. Eighteen bombers and six fighters fell burning into the Burmese countryside; over Rangoon, the jubilant pilots of No. 67 Squadron RAF accounted for twelve more.

Two P-40s were lost, but both pilots escaped. One of them, William E. Bartling, made a forced landing beside a railway line. Five minutes later, he was drinking a well-earned glass of beer in a railway coach, the mobile home of an English railroad overseer. The second pilot, Parker S. Dupouy, had a more traumatic experience. He shot down two bombers, then collided with a Zero in the ensuing mêlée. The Japanese fighter went spinning down, and Dupouy struggled back to base with four feet of wing missing. He walked away from the wreck of his P-40 with only a few bruises, but the fighter was a complete write-off.

The Japanese had taken a hammering, and the blow to their pride became apparent when, the following day, Tokyo Radio announced that if the AVG pilots at Rangoon persisted with their 'unorthodox tactics', they would be treated as guerrillas and shown no mercy if they fell into Japanese hands. It was clear that from now on the Japanese would exercise a great deal more caution when penetrating Burmese airspace. The P-40s, with their distinctive shark's-teeth nose markings, were opponents to be treated very seriously.

On 28 December, the Japanese dispatched a small force of fifteen bombers towards Rangoon. Ten P-40s were sent off to intercept them, but as soon as the fighters were sighted the enemy turned tail and fled. The P-40 pilots chased them across southern Burma until they were forced to land through lack of fuel at Moulmein. Then, while the bombers made their escape and the P-40s refuelled, the Japanese put the second part of their plan into operation. Ten more bombers, escorted by twenty Zeros, swept down on Mingaladon. Four P-40s and ten Buffaloes intercepted the enemy force forty miles south-east of Rangoon, but they were beaten off by the fighter escort and the bombers roared over the airfield at 3,000 feet, their bombs showering down to cause considerable damage to hangars, fuel dumps and grounded aircraft.

The Japanese returned the next day, and this time Rangoon itself was the target. Severe damage was inflicted on the railway station and the docks area, where large quantities of lend-lease equipment destined for China went up in flames. It seemed that the dwindling Allied fighter force was growing powerless to stem the enemy's air onslaught.

Then Bob Sandell's 1st Pursuit Squadron arrived from Kunming, joining Arivs Olsen's 3rd Squadron, and it was at that point that the balance was restored – at least for the time being. By this time the RAF's Buffaloes were virtually ineffective, having suffered serious losses, and the handful of survivors were withdrawn from the combat area.

"So," Sandell said, "we're really pleased to see you fellows. Maybe between us we can make the Japs think twice, even though we can't hope for air superiority. There are too many of them, too few of us. And our casualties aren't being replaced. We've given them a hammering, though."

Armstrong sucked thoughtfully on the stem of his unlit pipe.

"I was thinking about that," he said, "and even the Japanese can't go on sustaining casualties indefinitely in daylight attacks. It's my guess they'll switch to night raids, in which case we'll have a problem. Some of my chaps have got night-fighting experience, but that was mostly in Blenheims and Beaufighters, which were radar-equipped and had the benefit of a pretty good ground-control network, which doesn't exist here. There isn't any radar, for a start. Night fighting in a day fighter just isn't on. I tried it in a Hurricane, so I know. I managed to knock down the odd Jerry, but it was more by good luck than good judgement. I think we should brush up on our night flying, though, and keep a flight at readiness between dusk and dawn, just in case. We can take it in turns if you like."

"Okay." Sandell nodded in agreement. "By the way, Air Headquarters is sending some reinforcements. A squadron of RAF bombers, I understand. They should have been here by now. They were evacuated from Malaya to the Andaman Islands, and they were supposed to fly to us from there."

"Well, apparently the ground crews have turned up," Armstrong commented. "They arrived by sea in Rangoon yesterday, or so Flight Sergeant Cairns tells me. Apart from that, I don't know anything." Privately, he uttered an unspoken prayer that the bombers would be Hudsons, and not Blenheims. The prayer went unanswered.

Four

There was a Royal Air Force Medical Officer at Mingaladon. He was a flying officer, his name was Stephen Curtis, and he was an expert in tropical diseases. The fact that he was at Mingaladon was completely at variance with the RAF's normal procedures, which usually ensured that experts in tropical diseases were posted to the Outer Hebrides, while experts in hypothermia went to the Far East.

Not that it mattered much, Curtis thought, as he covertly surveyed the Hurricane pilots at readiness, sprawled in whatever shade they could find close to their aircraft. No matter how skilled one was, one couldn't function properly without medical supplies, which were practically non-existent. He had some quinine, for which he was thankful, because all these young men were going to go down with malaria sooner or later. The *burra sahibs* might keep it at arm's length with their mixture of blisteringly hot curries, gin and whisky – the theory being that no self-respecting mosquito would settle on them – but out here it was different, and in the jungle it was worse still.

There were other problems, too, evident in the drawn

features of the young flight lieutenant who had flown in from Singapore the day before, at the head of half a dozen Blenheim bombers. They were old Mark Ones, all that remained of the RAF bomber force that had fought its way step by step down the Malay peninsula, always just ahead of the advancing Japanese, until there was nowhere else to go but Singapore Island.

It was Flight Lieutenant Roger Craig and his crews who brought the first real news of how bad things had been in Malaya, and how bad they were now in Singapore. And once again, the men of Mingaladon had confirmation that the Japanese 'knew what they were up to.'

"On the first day of the attack, the eighth of December, they struck all our airfields in northern Malaya with fragmentation bombs," Craig said. "They wanted to keep the airfields intact for their own use later on, while at the same time inflicting as much damage as possible on our aircraft. They certainly did that. By the end of the second day our air strength in northern Malaya had been halved to about fifty aircraft."

Craig lit a fresh cigarette from the butt of the one he had just finished, a fact Curtis noted with some concern; but the medical officer said nothing. The Blenheim pilot was obviously keen to talk, to exorcise some of the demons he had brought with him.

"We found out that the Jap bombers were operating from Singora and Patani, in Siam," Craig continued, "so on the second or third day – I forget which – we scraped together all our available Blenheims for an attack on them. We hit Singora quite hard, but we lost five aircraft. Then, as we were preparing to take off on a second raid, the Japs appeared, bombed and strafed us at Butterworth, and knocked out all our Blenheims except one. It had taken off just a few seconds before the attack came in."

There was a long pause. A small lizard scurried up to Curtis's feet, went *chik-chik* in alarm as it surveyed the obstacle, then darted around it and scrabbled its way up a tent pole.

"Go on," the medical officer prompted.

"The pilot's name was Arthur Scarf," Craig said in a voice that was barely audible. "He was a flight lieutenant, a flight commander on Sixty-Two Squadron. I knew him pretty well. Anyway, he decided to press on alone to the target, which he attacked. Then the Jap fighters latched on to him, and chased him all the way to the Malayan border. He was badly wounded, but somehow he reached Alor Star airfield and made a forced landing. None of his crew was injured, but he . . . well, he died in hospital not long afterwards. The awful thing was, his wife was a nursing sister at Alor Star. She watched him die. If ever a man deserved a VC, it was Arthur Scarf."

There was another moody silence, during which Craig lit his third cigarette. Then he said:

"We received a trickle of replacement Blenheims, but we were reduced to operating them in ones and twos, trying to give a bit of help to our ground forces whenever we could. There were a few Buffaloes still left, but they were hopeless against the Japs and we used them mainly for reconnaissance and strafing. By the beginning of January we'd just about had it, and we were ordered to regroup on Singapore. That's when Crabtree and his pals joined us."

There were two more men in the tent. One was Bill Donahue, the war correspondent, who had furiously been making notes as Craig spoke (although he had no doubt that everything he wrote about the Malaya débâcle would be blue-pencilled by the censor); the other was a pilot officer with a heavily bandaged right arm. His name was Peter Crabtree, and he was one of half a dozen wounded aircrew who had been evacuated from Singapore by the Blenheims. Curtis had just changed his dressing and now, in much pain, he was sitting on a folding stool, drinking sugary tea. Donahue looked at him.

"Any chance of a few words from you, Peter, starting from square one?"

"I don't mind, as long as nobody else does," Crabtree said. "It'll help to take my mind off this." He looked down at his injured arm.

"Well, I suppose square one is July last year. That's when I first flew a Hurricane. It was at Ternhill in Shropshire, where I was awarded my wings and commissioned. I did some more hours on Hurricanes at the Operational Training Unit, Sutton Bridge, and then I was posted to an operational squadron – I'd better not say which one – with a grand total of a hundred and ninety flying hours, about seventy-five of them on Hurricanes. When I joined the squadron, preparations were already in hand for a move overseas, and we were all convinced that we were going to the Caucasus to give the Russians a hand."

Crabtree shifted his position on his stool, winced a little as a stab of pain troubled him, and took a swallow of tea.

"We had some pretty experienced pilots on the squadron. Our CO, who had formed the squadron in August, had eight confirmed kills in the Battle of Britain, and my flight commander had fought in France and the Battle of Britain before he was shot down and burnt; he was off flying for some months."

He smiled. "Things went ahead at a fairly leisurely pace until last November, when we received several new officers to fill specialist ground posts and about a dozen of our sergeant pilots were hastily commissioned to bring us up to overseas manning levels. Things got really hectic when our aircraft were fitted with long-range tanks and we practised very short take-offs, just in case we might have to fly from an aircraft carrier in the near future."

He was interrupted by a series of *chik-chiks*. The lizard had moved from its position at the top of the tent pole and, joined now by several more, was hanging upside down, its tiny claws clutching the tent canvas. The whole brood waited patiently for passing insects.

"He's obviously invited the family over for lunch," Crabtree grinned. "D'you want me to go on, or have you fallen asleep?"

The question was addressed to Donahue, who indicated that he was still wide awake.

"An advance party set out – six pilots, I think, with most of the ground officers and airmen – leaving twenty or so pilots kicking their heels at Padgate transit camp, awaiting a ship. We were told that we were to form a wing of four squadrons, and soon discovered that each squadron was to be commanded by an experienced CO, with equally experienced flight commanders leading teams of young pilots, most of whom had very little experience of operational flying and some of whom, like me, were completely raw.

"We sailed from the Clyde in a P. & O. cruise liner, the Strathallan, as part of a convoy of troopships bound for the Middle East. Whether we would ever have finished up fighting alongside the Russians we never found out, but about the middle of December – about a week after the Japs had attacked Pearl Harbor – we were told that we were being diverted to Singapore, where we were to be placed under General Wavell's Far East Command. The convoy ahead of us was also diverted; this carried the Eighteenth Infantry Division, as well as our advance party and fifty Hurricanes in crates."

Donahue, who of course had been in Malaya and Singapore and who had met Wavell, gave an involuntary grunt at the mention of his name. General Archibald Wavell, a very able commander who had led the Allied forces with distinction in the Western Desert before being transferred to his new command in south-east Asia, had one major fault; he held the Japanese soldier in contempt. In this view he was unshakeable, even when the Japanese were knocking on the gates of Singapore. It had proved to be a dangerous and fatal underestimation. So had Wavell's assumption that the young Indian troops now at his disposal, gallant yet completely untrained and unequipped for jungle warfare, were equals of the magnificent 4th and

5th Indian Divisions which had come under his command in North Africa.

The 16th Indian Brigade was a case in point. Early in January, in anticipation that the main Japanese threat in Burma would be likely to come from Raheng via Kawkareik, Paan and Kyaikto, and then Sittang, the 16th Indian Brigade under Brigadier K.J. Jones – a highly experienced Indian Army officer – had been despatched to Kawkareik with three battalions that had been milked to the last drop to send reinforcements to other theatres of war, and which had been brought up to strength with new and totally raw recruits only three days before the brigade embarked for Burma.

Donahue brought himself back to Crabtree's narrative and found himself starting to make meaningless strokes on his notepad, for most of the story he knew already – together with the numbers of the squadrons involved, which Crabtree had been reluctant to reveal in case the journalist turned out to be a Japanese agent.

The diverted supply convoy carrying the advance parties of the four squadrons, the troops and the Hurricanes had arrived in Singapore on 3 January 1942. At the same time, twenty more Hurricanes, fitted with long-range tanks, also arrived after flying from the aircraft carrier *Indomitable*. After being stripped of their extra fuel tanks and other non-essential equipment – anything that would reduce weight and improve their performance – they went into action from Kallang civil airport and, later, from the Changi road.

Even as the crated Hurricanes were being off-loaded,

Japanese troops were landing on the north shore of the Straits of Johore, opposite Singapore Island. Time was fast running out.

The Hurricanes earmarked for the defence of Singapore operated as No. 232 Squadron under Squadron Leader Llewellyn. The pilots fought on against mounting odds and scored some notable successes, such as on 20 January, when they destroyed eight of a formation of twenty-seven unescorted bombers over Singapore. The next day, however, the enemy bombers were escorted by the speedy Mitsubishi fighters – Navy Type 0s, or 'Zeros' as the Allies were beginning to call them – and this time five Hurricanes were shot down, with three pilots killed and the other two wounded. One of them was Crabtree.

Other gallant battles were still to be fought. At 1300 hours on 26 January, nine Vickers Vildebeests of No. 100 Squadron and three of No. 36, escorted by a small number of Hurricanes and Buffaloes, attempted to make a torpedo attack on transport ships supporting a Japanese landing at Endau, in southern Malaya. The Vildebeests, lumbering biplanes with a top speed of only 150 miles per hour, were no match for the Japanese fighters that came up to intercept them. Scattering the British fighter escort, they shot down five of the torpedo bombers.

Worse was to come. Two hours later, nine Vildebeests of No. 36 Squadron made a second attack. All nine failed to return.

"A couple of days after that," Crabtree said, "only twenty Hurricanes were still airworthy, and only about ten of those were serviceable at any one time. The number of

Buffaloes was down to six. The condition of the remaining airfields didn't help our problems, either. Most of the labour force had disappeared, so it was left to our airmen and the troops to fill in bomb craters, and at Kallang, which was built on reclaimed ground, sticky mud oozed up through the holes and flowed across the airstrip."

"That was when they decided to evacuate what was left of the bomber force," Craig interjected. "In any case, there wasn't much point in staying in Singapore; we had no bombs left. Most of the Blenheims and Hudsons went to Sumatra, and I was detailed to bring half a dozen Blenheims here."

He got up and walked out into the open air, looking at the recumbent Hurricane pilots and then at the sky. "Not a lot going on," he remarked. I wonder what the bastards are up to?"

That question might have been readily answered by the crew of a Japanese aircraft which, at that very moment and completely unseen, was cruising at an altitude of 25,000 feet over Mingaladon. Twin-engined, extremely fast and very streamlined, it was a Mitsubishi Ki-46 reconnaissance aircraft. Its top speed was over 370 miles per hour, which made it a good 50 miles per hour faster than either the Hurricane or the P-40; it could climb to over 35,000 feet, which neither the Hurricane nor the P-40 could do; and it could stay airborne for six hours, in which time it could cover a distance of 1,300 miles at cruising speed.

From the summer of 1941, when the first examples were delivered to the Japanese Army Air Force, Ki-46 detachments had flown combat missions over China and the whole of south-east Asia, ranging as far west as the Bay of Bengal. As yet, the Allies had no idea that such an aircraft existed.

The aircraft that flew high over Mingaladon on this second day of February 1942, had done so every day for the past week, as well as photographing Rangoon. Its cameras would reveal the extent of the fighter force based there, as well as the fact that bombers had also arrived.

Moulmein and other airstrips in Tenasserim were now in Japanese hands; this would enable Japanese fighters to escort the bombers all the way to Rangoon and beyond. The way was now clear for the Army Air Force to launch an all-out attack aimed at destroying the Allies' puny air power, paving the way for the unopposed battering of Rangoon that would be the prelude to the crossing of the Sittang river by the Japanese Army, which would then advance in triumph on the Burmese capital, sweeping all before it.

It never occurred to the Japanese that the Allies, puny or not, might decide to strike the first blow.

Five

Pre-Dawn, 3 February 1942

The management of the Mingaladon Golf Club had given up. The whole of the RAF, not to mention the Americans, seemed to have moved within its hallowed walls since the last Japanese attack on the airfield had destroyed more of its facilities. Now a couple of dozen boisterous young men had virtually taken over the place. They slept on beds and benches all over the big, cool lounge where once the *burra sahibs* and their ladies had sipped iced drinks after golf on Saturday afternoons; they had long conversations with the Burmese and Indian waiters, which was absolutely unheard of and contrary to every rule; they drank the club's bar dry and smoked its stocks of cigarettes – all of which, admittedly, they paid for; and, the final sacrilege, they lay shirtless on the lawn in front of the clubhouse, sunning themselves.

The RAF cookhouse staff, their field kitchens blasted to smithereens in the air raid (for which act, in the opinion of most, the Japanese bomb aimer responsible should have received an immediate award) had now moved into the clubhouse kitchen, from where they dispensed food on a twice-daily basis. Those who could afford it purchased breakfast from the Golf Club, and had two fried eggs and bacon, toast and marmalade; those who could not had to put up with the unvaried RAF breakfast fare of two sausages, swimming in grease astride a wooden slice of fried bread, followed by two pieces of unbuttered bread and a spoonful of watery jam. Luckily, there was plenty of tea to wash it down.

Armstrong, who had been preoccupied with other matters since his arrival in Burma, promised himself that he would give his urgent attention to the food problem. The cookhouse staff were lazy, as was the warrant officer in charge of them, and there was more than a hint that the man might be selling off rations. Whatever was going on, the food was inexcusable. The market in Rangoon was still well stocked with meat and vegetables, and some of it should be coming the way of his pilots and ground crews. The Americans had their own source of supply, part of which they donated to their less fortunate RAF counterparts. Americans living in Rangoon, mostly employees of the General Motors Corporation who were there to supervise the assembly of lease-lend vehicles, had organised a supply line that ensured a steady flow of food, iced beer, chocolate, cakes and cigarettes to the Volunteer Group.

It was 0330. In an hour or so, Indian water-carriers would descend on the club to begin their daily task of watering the greens, on which the few remaining members still played a round or two. Before the arrival of the RAF and AVG, a club servant had summoned them by hammering loudly on a piece of suspended steel railway track; the practice had ceased abruptly after a person or persons unknown, jerked unceremoniously from exhausted sleep, had threatened the man with a slow and painful death.

Today, sleep was for later. The aircrews had forced down an early breakfast and were now assembling in the club foyer, waiting for the trucks that would take them to the airfield. All had been fully briefed on the forthcoming mission.

For the past twenty-four hours – according to reports filtered back by patrols of the 1/7th Gurkha Rifles, skirmishing with the Japanese in the Moulmein area – the enemy had been flying bombers and fighters into the airfield there. If all went well, they were in for a nasty surprise.

Armstrong, Sandell, Arivs Olson and Roger Craig had worked out the details. The Hurricanes, once again fitted with their long-range fuel tanks, would go in first. Armstrong had picked eleven pilots, plus himself; six less experienced men and their aircraft would remain at Mingaladon as a Battle Flight in case the Japanese raided Rangoon. Five minutes after the Hurricanes strafed Moulmein, Craig's six Blenheims, armed with American 250-pound bombs – which were not in short supply – would make their attack; then twelve P-40s, six each from the 1st and 3rd Pursuit Squadrons, would make one strafing run before joining up with the Blenheims to escort them home.

"Let's hope we can really shake 'em up, Sandy," Armstrong said, as the truck disgorged them at the airfield.

"Maybe we can buy ourselves a bit of time until more reinforcements arrive."

"Well, we certainly tickled 'em up at Raheng," Sandell said with a grin. "Seems we hit the place on the very day the Japs were trying to impress the Siamese. Apparently they had invited a number of local dignitaries along to watch their bombers take off on a sortie, have a spot of lunch, then watch them come back again. What we did to them was reported in the Bangkok newspapers the next day, so I'm led to believe. I'll bet the Jap censors had a fit."

Joined by Olson and Craig, they made a final check of the navigational details. They were simple enough; the shortest route to Moulmein was straight across the Gulf of Martaban, about a hundred miles. The plan was to bypass the airfield at low level and then turn to hit it from the east, out of the rising sun.

"With any luck we'll catch the Japs with their asses in the air, making their ceremonial bow as they raise the flag," Arivs Olson said. He glanced towards the east, where a streak of pale green was rapidly expanding on the horizon. The sun would rise in about forty-five minutes. It was time to go.

All the Hurricanes took off without incident and headed out over the coast, keeping low and flying in three sections of four. Armstrong had quickly adopted the 'finger four' battle formation used by the Americans; he was leading Red Section, with Baird following him at the head of Blue and Kalinski bringing up the rear with Yellow.

The muddy waters of the gulf sped beneath their wings,

which now bore different markings. The previous day, orders had come down from Allied Command HQ at Akyab that the red was to be deleted from the RAF roundel, for fear of confusion with the Japanese 'meatball', as the AVG pilots had nicknamed the enemy's national insignia. The ground crews had spent hours painting over the red part, so that the end result was a white disc surrounded by a blue circle. Armstrong didn't like the idea at all; the white disc would be easy to pick out by the pilot of an aircraft flying higher up, especially against a dark green jungle background.

After half an hour's flying they crossed the coast of Tenasserim a few miles to the south of Moulmein, flew on towards Kawkareik, then turned left and headed back towards the airfield. Behind them now, the red ball of the rising sun turned the sky crimson, shot with streaks of green and gold. Its reflection glowed on the inside of their windscreens, and on the wings and fuselages of the Japanese fighters and bombers that were now clearly visible on the aerodrome ahead.

Armstrong ordered the three sections to attack in line abreast. Right in front of his own Hurricane an aircraft was taking off, and his mind swiftly registered its details. It was a monoplane, with a radial engine and a retractable undercarriage; he saw the latter starting to come up as the aircraft grew larger in his gunsight. Ruddering slightly to give himself the necessary deflection, he fired a short burst and saw sparks fly from the enemy's engine cowling as it struck home. Almost at once, the aircraft lost flying speed; its wingtip hit the ground and it cartwheeled in a great arc, ploughing through a row of parked bombers and exploding among some canvas hangars.

Armstrong sped over the bombers, firing as he went, and pulled up in a steep climbing turn, looking back. Columns of flame-shot smoke were beginning to rise from wrecked aircraft; other machines were beginning to taxi out, and he identified them as the same type as the one he had shot down. He pressed the R/T button.

"Red Leader to all sections. We're going in again. Red Section, let's get those fighters. Blue and Yellow, concentrate on the bombers!"

The Hurricanes swept across the airfield a second time. Armstrong, closing in on a fighter that was just starting its take-off run, regretted that the gun cameras had been removed from the aircraft as part of the weight-saving exercise, and tried to stamp a mental picture of the enemy aircraft on his mind so that he could make a sketch of it later on. Its wheels left the ground and it immediately went into a shallow climb, giving him a good look at its silhouette. Stubby radial engine, broad wings with rounded tips and a marked forward sweep at the trailing edge . . . a long, slender rear fuselage ending in a single fin and rudder.

A moment later, the image shuddered and disintegrated as eight streams of bullets converged on it just behind the cockpit and the fighter tore apart. Its starboard wing broke off and whirled away in the slipstream, flashing just past Armstrong's wingtip; the rest, a blazing mass, gyrated away in the opposite direction. He did not see it crash, being too intent now on dodging the machine-gun fire that came at him from various points on the ground. He felt, rather than heard, several loud cracks and knew that his aircraft had been hit, but a glance at his instruments and the response of the controls reassured him that everything was working properly.

"All sections, form up and stay low. Let's go home. Check in, everybody."

They all did, except for Yellow Four, who appeared to have flown into the ground as he was machine-gunning a row of bombers. Yellow Four: that was a young sergeant pilot named Balfour, who had joined the squadron just before it left Egypt. He had seen action over Greece and Crete. It seemed somehow unfair that he should end his days here, in this unknown land.

As they flew back over the Gulf of Martaban, Armstrong pondered over the enemy fighters he had destroyed, and came to two possible conclusions. Either they were the Type 0 fighters, the 'Zeros' the AVG pilots had told him about and which had caused such havoc with the RAF squadrons in Malaya, or they were a development of the little Nakajima fighters, with their fixed undercarriages, which the Allies had encountered in considerable numbers over Burma.

Some time later, to his great relief, all six Blenheims returned safely to Mingaladon, their crews jubilant, closely followed by the twelve P-40s.

"You really did the trick, sir," a flushed and excited Craig told him as he climbed down from the bomber, his khaki tropical uniform soaked in damp patches of sweat. "Not one Jap fighter came up – not one! We hit the target right on the nose and then we saw the Americans making their attack through the smoke. A few more raids like that, and we'll stop them in their tracks!"

I doubt it, Armstrong told himself grimly, although he smiled and nodded at Craig's enthusiasm. The successful attack had provided a much-needed tonic for the young bomber pilot and his crews.

Armstrong remembered that he needed to make some drawings of the unidentified Japanese fighters; he now did so, with some help from Baird and Kalinski, and then went off to confer with the Americans. Sandell looked at the sketches closely and passed them to his colleagues, shaking his head slowly.

"The only ones we saw at Moulmein were in little bits," he said, "but they definitely weren't Zeros. These are too angular; the Zero's lines are softer, and the wing shape is all wrong."

"Maybe it's this 'Type One Retractable Gear Fighter' we've been hearing about, Sandy." The speaker was Arivs Olson, who was inspecting Armstrong's drawings closely.

Sandell nodded. "Maybe. You know, I've been thinking. It would make our lives a lot easier if we applied code names to these Jap ships. We could call this fellow 'Jim', for example."

They laughed.

"No, no," Sandell persisted, "I'm serious! It makes enormous sense. With one or two exceptions we have no idea how the Japanese designate their aircraft, so we're condemned to using cumbersome expressions like the one Arivs just coughed out. I've been giving some thought to this, as a matter of fact. Suppose, say, we applied boys' names to the Jap fighters, and girls' names to the bomber types. That would provide a simple, and to my mind effective, means of identification. What do you think, Ken?"

"I'm all for it," Armstrong said, "especially if a lot of different types are involved. At least we knew where we were with the Germans and Italians, even though they used numbers – like the Me 109 and Ju 88 – rather than names. Even then, we got it wrong sometimes. During the Battle of Britain, the Jerries put it about that they had a new type of fighter, called the Heinkel 113, in service in large numbers. All of a sudden, every RAF fighter pilot was meeting He 113s over England and shooting them down. The funny thing was, we never found the wreckage of one, and we eventually found out why via various intelligence sources. Heinkel only ever built a few prototypes, which the Jerries camouflaged and painted in fake squadron markings. We fell for it hook, line and sinker."

"Well," Sandell said, "I intend to put my idea down in writing and submit it to Air Command. You never know – just for once, they might take notice. I doubt it, but it's worth a try."

A hundred miles away, the mysterious aircraft that was giving rise to so much speculation among the Allied fighter pilots was foremost in the thoughts of a certain Lieutenant-Colonel Ozawa. He was the base commander at Moulmein, and now, as he surveyed the devastation caused by the Allied raid, he permitted himself a thin smile. It was an outward sign of the emotion he felt, and it had nothing to do with humour. A westerner would have been weeping.

Japan's latest army fighter, the Nakajima Ki-43 *Hayabusa* – the aptly named Peregrine Falcon – had been entrusted to his care. A whole squadron had been deployed to Moulmein for operations over Burma, where they were to have swept the Allied fighters and bombers from the skies.

Now only two remained. The rest were twisted wrecks from which columns of smoke rose. Ozawa thought that the columns looked like accusing fingers, directed at him. Nor was that all. Half of the available bomber force, now commanded by Tanaka since Watanabe's death, also lay in ruins. He did not care to contemplate the wrath that would descend on him, when his superiors in Bangkok reacted to the disaster.

His own wrath had already fallen on the man responsible for Moulmein's air defences, a young lieutenant who had been an accountant before the war, and who had been chastised on several occasions for his lack of military bearing.

The lieutenant now sat cross-legged on a mat in his quarters, naked from the waist up, gazing at the ceremonial knife in his hand. Just behind him and a little to one side a brother officer stood, feet apart, grasping the long hilt of a razor-sharp samurai sword with both hands.

It was time. Gulping in fear of the unknown, the lieutenant breathed a prayer to his ancestors, begging their forgiveness, and plunged the knife into the left-hand side of his stomach, dragging the blade horizontally through the quivering flesh. He felt no pain, only a strange numbness. Then he looked down at the spurting blood, the gushing entrails, and a scream of pure horror rose within him.

It never reached his lips. The samurai sword flashed down in the mercy stroke, cleanly severing the lieutenant's head from his body.

The officer carefully wiped the blade, then, leaving some orderlies to clean up the mess, went to report to Ozawa.

"It is done, then?" Ozawa said, as the officer came to attention before him and gave a little bow, saluting as he did so.

"It is done, sir."

"Very well. Dismissed."

Ozawa turned and stared eastwards through the clouds of drifting smoke. There was hatred in his eyes, and he made a solemn vow to his particular gods. Those round-eyed, pale-skinned bastards would pay for this day's work. And soon.

Six

Night Action, 15 February, 1942

Bob Sandell was dead. On 9 February, he had taken off to carry out an air test in a newly repaired P-40. What actually happened no one knew, but eyewitnesses told how the fighter appeared to enter a roll at low altitude and dive into the ground. Small, quietly spoken Sandell was killed instantly. He had five enemy aircraft to his credit. His place was taken by Squadron Leader Robert H. Neale, whose first, unenviable task was to lay plans for the eventual evacuation of the AVG from the Rangoon area, a move that seemed increasingly likely as the situation on the ground continued to deteriorate.

But that time was not yet, and in the meantime the Japanese, having altered their tactics, were attacking more frequently at night, as Armstrong had predicted they would.

At first, Armstrong was reluctant to risk his pilots and aircraft – only a dozen of which were now serviceable – in night operations. The flarepath facilities at Mingaladon were practically non-existent, and only a few of his pilots had night-fighting experience. Fewer still had flown single-engined day fighters in combat at night. But as the attacks on Rangoon were stepped up, and morale among the capital's civilian population hit rock bottom, he knew that he was going to have to do something. So did Bob Neale, even though his superiors had flatly forbidden the AVG pilots to fly at night after three precious P-40s had been written off in landing accidents.

On the previous night, Armstrong and Neale had stood outside the Mingaladon Golf Club and listened to the distant hum of Japanese aero-engines. As it grew louder, the sirens in Rangoon began to wail and desultory anti-aircraft fire spattered the sky. The crump of explosions followed soon after, the flashes of the bombs lighting up the skyline. A few bombers passed overhead, the red pinpoints of their engine exhausts clearly visible; the Japanese had attacked from a fairly low altitude to make certain of hitting their target, the docks area of the city.

At that moment, Armstrong decided that he had had enough. He was going to have a crack at the night bombers. The moon was nearly full, which was an advantage. Having made up his mind, he went to bed and slept soundly until first light, and after breakfast he sought out his Polish flight commander, Stanislaw Kalinski, and told him about his plan. Like himself, Kalinski had also flown single-engined fighters on night operations. Armstrong had briefly toyed with the idea of committing all his experienced pilots, but had decided it would be foolish to risk their necks in what, after all, might turn out to be an abortive operation.

The two pilots spent all day discussing the best chance of intercepting the enemy bombers. The first priority was to make sure they had adequate warning of the bombers' approach, so Armstrong got 'Sticky' Glew to contact his chain of ground observers to make sure that they would be on full alert.

"The bombers come in at about eight thousand feet," Armstrong pointed out, "and sometimes much lower than that. But let's say eight thousand. We need to be at ten or twelve thousand, which means that we've got to be airborne for at least ten minutes after we get the first warning, if we are going to intercept them before they reach Rangoon. It looks like being a clear night, with a good moon, so we should be able to spot them easily enough."

In the afternoon they taxied their Hurricanes to a position close to the control tent, where they would wait for news of the incoming raiders, then went off to have a meal and snatch a little sleep. Glew and the two ground crews detailed by Flight Sergeant Cairns did the same; it could be a long night, with nothing to show at the end of it if the Japanese failed to turn up.

A few hours later, as they dozed in the control tent while Glew yawned beside his radio, his eyes willing the warning telephone to ring, Armstrong and Kalinski were wondering if they were wasting their time. Two o'clock came and went, and they were now in that peculiar time-zone of the small hours where humans are at their lowest ebb. To protect their night vision the tent was in complete darkness; Armstrong was dying for a smoke, but did not dare light his pipe.

"The Japs have never been as late as this, Stan,"

Armstrong said. "I think we'll give it another half-hour, then call it a night."

"Maybe our friendly *nats* are off duty," Kalinski commented. The others chuckled. Every native of Burma believed in *nats*, or fairies; the pilots had taken to the idea, first as a joke, but as time went by some of the more superstitious had begun to believe there might be something in it.

"I was talking to the guy who runs the bakery in Rangoon the other day," Glew said. "Tells me that most of his customers are convinced that you fellas are *nats* in human form, protecting their city. Some of them really do think you're supernatural, you know. Hold you in absolute awe."

"That's a hell of a reputation to live up to," Kalinski grunted, standing up to stretch his limbs. "A bit of divine intervention is what we need, I reckon. Not to mention a few more squadrons of Hurricanes and P-40s and some Beaufighters."

The telephone at Glew's elbow rang. He grabbed the receiver, then gave an ear-splitting yell.

"Air raid! Twenty plus, heading for Rangoon!"

Armstrong and Kalinski collided with one another in their haste to get to their aircraft, swore, sorted themselves out and hurled themselves into their cockpits. The ground crews were standing by and in a couple of minutes both Merlin engines were running smoothly.

They took off in the moonlight, the flarepath unlit on Armstrong's instructions. Dim and barely effective though it was, on a clear night like this it would be seen from miles away, and would tell the Japanese that fighters were coming up to intercept them. They had their radios tuned in to the usual frequency in case Glew needed to pass urgent information on to them, but they would maintain radio silence until they were among the bombers, when it would no longer matter.

Armstrong reached 12,000 feet and throttled back, combing the sky in wide circles. Kalinski was still some distance below, having taken off a couple of minutes later. The engine roared steadily and the radio's carrier wave hissed and crackled in his headphones.

Suddenly, Glew's distorted voice burst over the airwaves. "Bandits approaching Elephant Point, heading north-north-west!"

Elephant Point – that meant the bombers had made a detour out to sea and were now heading straight up the estuary of the Irrawaddy River, making for the docks.

Armstrong came out of his turn and opened the throttle again, pointing the Hurricane's nose towards the estuary, twisting his head from side to side as he peered down, trying to spot the elusive enemy. The waters of the estuary were silver in the moonlight; anything flying over them should have stuck out like a sore thumb. Yet there was nothing.

Baffled, Armstrong slid back the cockpit hood in order to get a better look. As he did so, he saw a pinprick of light above him and at first thought it was a star; but the stars were blotted out by the light of the moon. He looked again, striving to relax his eyes, and this time there was no mistake. There was not one light, but two;

bright blue-white glimmers that told him he was seeing an aircraft's engine exhausts.

He made an urgent radio call to Kalinski, not bothering with the callsign – Sonata – which they had agreed upon.

"Stan, they're above us! I am attacking now – watch out for my fire. I'm right under their formation."

Armstrong could now pick out more twin sets of exhaust lights. Pushing the throttle wide open, he selected a bomber – the first he had detected – and began a climbing right turn that would bring him into position astern of it. At all costs, he had to keep his eyes on it. He wanted to nail it, to break up the enemy formation before it reached the city.

The distance between the Hurricane and the bomber was closing rapidly. The pinprick lights of its exhausts were growing larger now, and becoming brighter by the second. He had now climbed to 15,000 feet and saw that he was astern of the left-hand aircraft of a formation of three; the dark silhouettes of the enemy aircraft were clearly visible. The moon was off to the right. His thumb hovered over the gun button. Just a little closer . . .

Damn! His target's left wing suddenly rose as the bomber turned to the right. The other two were also turning, making a last course correction as they ran in towards their objective. The manoeuvre took Armstrong by surprise and his fighter slid out to the left, opening up the distance. He corrected quickly, steadying the Hurricane again as he closed in for the kill.

The Hurricane carried 2,600 rounds of mixed tracer and armour-piercing 0.303-inch ammunition. With the bomber in his sights, 250 yards ahead of him, Armstrong touched the gun button and held it down for two seconds. In that time, 266 bullets, the whole mass of metal weighing twenty pounds and the tracer among it glowing white-hot, converged on that exact spot where the bomber hung in space and punched a lethal hole, like a charge of buckshot fired at close range, through its thin skin where the starboard wing root joined the fuselage.

The effect was instantaneous. Black smoke and oil poured back from the bomber, which wavered but held its course as its pilot strove to keep it in the air until he completed his bombing run. He was fighting a losing battle. Armstrong, ignoring return fire that was now lancing at him, fired again and suddenly one of the bomber's wing tanks exploded in a searing yellow ball of flame. Its nose went down abruptly and it fell earthwards in a spiral dive, breaking up as it went. Armstrong, not yet familiar with the Japanese code of honour, wondered why there were no parachutes. There had been time for crew members to escape.

He was suddenly conscious of flickering light flashes off to his right. Not until his aircraft was subjected to a succession of hammer-blows did he become fully aware that he was under attack. Tracer bullets seemed to be coming at him from all directions; he must be slap in the middle of a box of bombers. A glance told him that there was nothing below and he headed downhill fast, out of the enemy fire that groped for him.

The altimeter unwound quickly. He levelled out a few thousand feet above the estuary and was about to climb back up for a second attack when he became conscious of a strong smell of burning. He couldn't tell where it was coming from, but he was glad that he had left his cockpit hood open; that would save a vital couple of seconds if he had to part company with the aircraft.

On the shore of the estuary, the Burmese commander of an anti-aircraft battery spotted Armstrong's aircraft as it cruised towards Rangoon, and saw what Armstrong could not see: a comet-like tail of flame, trailing in the Hurricane's wake.

The aircraft was clearly Japanese, the battery commander thought, and gave the order to open fire. The shooting was surprisingly good.

Ahead of Armstrong, a bright flash filled the sky. The engine gave a loud bang and stopped. Dazed and momentarily blinded, he sensed the aircraft starting to drop, shook his head to clear it, squeezed his eyes tightly shut and then opened them again, peering at the altimeter. It read 1,500 feet.

Armstrong trimmed the aircraft to glide. It was becoming uncomfortably hot in the cockpit and the pilot now knew for certain that the Hurricane was on fire. He had no alternative other than to ditch in the estuary; he was now too low to bale out safely.

Oil on his windscreen was making it increasingly impossible to see ahead. He knew that he had to get down quickly. At least, he thought, he didn't have to worry about such factors as sea states, waves and the like; the estuary was as calm as a millpond. Too calm, perhaps, for it would be difficult to judge his true height above the water in the last second or two, when the altimeter became useless.

He made sure that the cockpit canopy was locked in the fully back position – an unlocked hood could give a pilot a nasty crack on the head if it suddenly slid forward – and tightened his straps. He had already switched everything off, so all he had to do now was to concentrate on the ditching procedure.

The waters of the estuary were rising up to enfold him. Breathing a silent prayer that the *nats* of the river were in a good mood, he eased back progressively on the stick. The Hurricane shuddered as its tail made contact with the surface, braking the fighter gently. It was the perfect tail-down ditching – or it would have been, had not the Hurricane struck some unseen obstacle and broken apart in a fearsome cacophony of sound.

Armstrong was vaguely conscious of the scream of rending metal and wood, and of a huge mass of water cascading over the cockpit. The brutal deceleration momentarily stunned him, but his tight straps held his body in place, although a fierce pain in his neck told him that he might have a whiplash injury to contend with.

His immediate problem was that the engine was dragging the cockpit section – with himself still strapped into it – down to the muddy depths of the Irrawaddy. He groped for his seat harness release, managed to unfasten it, and tried to push himself up out of the cockpit. The water was over his head and he was holding his breath. Something was still holding him in the cockpit and he began to panic until he realised that it was the weight of his parachute pack. Reaching down, he turned the metal disc of the quick release mechanism and gave it a sharp punch. Flicking the shoulder straps aside, he placed both hands on the cockpit sides and heaved.

A couple of seconds later, having made his exit from the cockpit like a cork out of a bottle, he found himself bursting through the surface, taking great gulps of air, which smelt wonderful, and spitting out copious quantities of muddy water, which tasted horrible.

Treading water, he inflated his Mae West life-jacket and looked around. A patch of burning fuel some distance away told him where the other half of his aircraft had gone down.

"Bloody river *nats*," he said fervently, then told himself that he might be tempting fate, for he was not yet out of their territory.

The Japanese bombers had unloaded their bombs on Rangoon and were now heading for home, the beat of their engines far overhead. Wondering if Kalinski had had any luck, Armstrong began to swim towards the shore, aware that the current – which was quite strong – might well carry him out to sea before help could reach him. He had no difficulty in getting his bearings, for much of the shoreline seemed to be on fire.

Swimming was hard work – he was restricted to a back-stroke because of the encumbrance of his life-jacket – and Armstrong was a poor swimmer at the best of times. He ached all over, he felt sick, and he soon began to tire. He could feel the current tugging at him all the while, and the fires on shore seemed to be getting no nearer.

After half an hour he was becoming exhausted, and his mind was beginning to wander. There was a bright light, stabbing into his brain. It ebbed away, to be replaced once more by darkness, then returned, brighter than ever. There were excited voices, the chug-chug of a boat's engine. Something was tugging at his Mae West. Hands, none too gentle, were grasping him under the armpits and hauling him from the water. He landed face-down on the wooden planking of a boat's deck. It stank of oil, fish and urine.

Someone kicked him hard in the ribs and a voice screamed "*Japani! Japani!*"

"Not *Japani*, silly bastard. English! RAF!" he thought he heard himself saying, just before he passed out.

He awoke to the cleansing smell of carbolic soap and disinfectant. Not caring where he was, he lay there, savouring the aromas, and kept his eyes shut for a few moments. At length, he opened them cautiously, only to shut them again quickly. It was as though someone had thrown a mixture of powdered glass and pepper into them.

"Lie still," a voice ordered. A female voice. "This won't take a minute."

His eyelids were being gently bathed, massaged by what felt like cotton wool impregnated with a cool liquid that stung slightly. He wanted the soothing sensation to last for a long time. Instead, it ceased.

"All right," the unseen owner of the voice said. "Try to open them now."

He did so, and this time the painful prickling was bearable. His eyes stayed open, registering the fact that

94

he was in a bed of some sort, in a room of some sort, and that daylight was flooding in through a window.

A face swam into focus. It was oval-shaped, with wide-set eyes (brown? green? Later, he could not remember) and a nose that was just a bit too large. It was topped by a white nurse's cap, or bonnet, or whatever one called it, and its chin rested on a white starched collar above a grey blouse. Its mouth, wide, like the eyes, smiled at him.

"That's better. Now, let's see if we can get you off your back."

An arm inserted itself between the bed and his shoulders and slowly raised his torso. He felt a couple of pillows being tucked behind his back, and winced as pain plucked at his muscles. His neck felt as though it were being stretched.

"Yes, you'll feel it for a while," the nurse told him in what he thought was an unduly cheerful tone. "You've got some bad bruising, but there's no serious damage. You were lucky, Wing Commander."

"What happened?" he asked, his voice a harsh croak. His throat hurt and he raised a hand to his larynx.

"We had to pump you out," the nurse said. "You'd swallowed a lot of river water, and it's not the world's cleanest. Don't you recall anything?"

Armstrong frowned, which made his face hurt. "I remember the Hurricane breaking up when I ditched," he said laboriously, "and then there was a bright light. Must have been a searchlight, I suppose. Then some people pulled me out of the water. I think they thought

I was Japanese," he added, a dull ache in his rib cage jogging his memory.

"You were picked up by the crew of a Burmese Navy river boat," the nurse informed him. "Once they had established who you were, they brought you into Rangoon by way of the Twante Canal, which links the Irrawaddy with the Rangoon river, and had you rushed here. You were out cold all the while."

"Where's here?" Armstrong wanted to know.

"Mingaladon Hospital. You dropped in at just the right time. The previous occupant of your bed was a Burmese general with piles, which is why this is a private room. We discharged him and his sore bottom yesterday. There are some British officers in the ward down the corridor, though, recovering from wounds. Perhaps you'd care to drop in on them later, when you're feeling better. I'll bring you some soup later on. In the meantime, drink as much of that as you can." She indicated a jug of iced water that stood on the bedside locker, and turned to leave.

"What shall I call you?" Armstrong asked suddenly. She half turned in the doorway.

"Sister Windrush," she said. "Philippa Windrush. By the way, your uniform is being cleaned and pressed."

Armstrong relaxed against his pillows, forgetting his aches and pains for a moment. Philippa Windrush, he thought. Sounds like a heroine out of girls' story-book. Still, attractive enough. And the nurse's uniform somehow added to the attraction.

It was not Philippa Windrush who brought him the promised soup – which was actually beef broth – but a smiling Burmese orderly. He also brought a walking stick and Armstrong's clean uniform. Feeling a good deal better after he had eaten, Armstrong dressed with some difficulty and then hobbled off along the corridor in search of the British officers. There were four of them, all Army men, and he found them sitting around a small table on the veranda, smoking and playing cards. Armstrong had discovered from the Burmese orderly that they had all been injured during the fighting in Tenasserim.

They glanced at Armstrong as he sat down close by, acknowledged his presence with curt greetings, then returned to their game. The pilot felt irritated.

"Something troubling you chaps?" he asked sharply.

One of the officers, a lieutenant with a livid red scare down the right side of his face, looked at him insolently.

"Well, *sir*," he said, uttering the word in a derisory manner, "the Japs troubled us a lot, as a matter of fact. Might have troubled us a lot less, though, if the RAF had showed up from time to time."

Armstrong felt his anger rising and was about to make a reply when he suddenly realised it wasn't worth it. He had come across exactly the same attitude after Dunkirk, and he couldn't really blame the troops, who must have gone through hell. No explanation in the world would satisfy men who had been on the receiving end of continual air attack, and who had seen few, if any, of their own aircraft. Instead, he said:

"Has anyone got a cigarette? I left my pipe and tobacco behind when I took off last night."

One of the other Army officers looked at him with

sudden interest and passed him a pack of cigarettes. Armstrong took one and accepted a light.

"Were you in action against the Jap night bombers, sir? We watched that. We're supposed to use the slit trenches when there's a raid on, you know, but we never do. Had enough of slit trenches, haven't we, chaps?"

Armstrong nodded, but made no comment. The cigarette tasted foul, but he went on smoking it nonetheless.

"We saw at least three planes going down in flames," the Army officer went on. "Lit up the sky for miles around. Were you shot down yourself?"

Armstrong nodded again. "Regrettably, yes. I had to ditch in the estuary. Got a bomber first, though," he added, rather self-consciously. So Kalinski must have got the other two, he thought, unless one of the flaming aircraft – perish the idea – had been the Pole's Hurricane.

He was suddenly aware that he hadn't even thought about telephoning the airfield, which was inexcusable. Stubbing out his half-smoked cigarette, he levered himself out of his chair and was about to go off in search of a phone when Sister Windrush put in an appearance, closely followed by two men. With immense relief, Armstrong saw that one was Kalinski; the other was Dickie Baird.

"You have visitors, Wing Commander," Sister Windrush said quietly. Armstrong noticed that she was not smiling. Neither were his two fellow officers.

"We are glad to see you're okay," Kalinski said. His face was grim.

"Well," Armstrong said wryly, "you don't seem too pleased about it. What's up with the pair of you?"

"You won't have heard, Ken. The news came in just a while ago." It was Baird who spoke.

"The Japs have taken Singapore."

Seven

The end in Singapore had come quickly. The final battle began on the night of 7 February, when a battle group of the Japanese Guards Division landed on Ubin Island, in the eastern part of the Johore Strait. On the following day the city came under heavy bombardment from the air and the guns of the Japanese 25th Army, and on 9 February the Japanese 5th and 18th Infantry Divisions crossed the Johore Strait, followed by the Guards Division. Supported by two armoured regiments, the Japanese forced the British and Australian defenders back into Singapore city itself.

On the fifteenth, the British commander in Singapore, Lieutenant-General Percival, ordered his troops to lay down their arms; 130,000 troops were taken prisoner. It was the biggest single defeat in British history.

The surviving bombers and fighters – all except Flight Lieutenant Craig's six Blenheims, which went to Burma via the Andamans – were evacuated to Java, as was a remnant of forces that had striven vainly to defend Singapore. But it was in the neighbouring island of Sumatra that the next line of resistance was planned.

The first fighter reinforcements to arrive in Sumatra, late in January 1942, were forty-eight Hurricane Mk IIAs, which the aircraft carrier *Indomitable* had collected at Aden. On 26 January they were flown off by a mixture of pilots drawn from Nos. 242, 258 and 605 Squadrons, all of whom had originally been destined for Singapore. The aircraft were dispersed between PI, an airstrip at Palembang, and PII, a new and secret strip further south. Unfortunately, five of the Hurricanes crashed on landing at Palembang, and because their guns were choked with anti-corrosion grease and had to be stripped and cleaned, it was some time before the remainder could go into action.

Conditions on Sumatra were appalling, with airfields severely congested and their surfaces in a fearful state as a result of the heavy rains. The task of the air units in Sumatra became doubly difficult after 14 February, when the Japanese launched a heavy attack on Palembang airstrip. Soon afterwards, a formation of twin-engined aircraft droned towards the base; they looked exactly like Lockheed Hudsons, and many of the defenders cheered. But the aircraft were Japanese Kawasaki Ki-56 transports – which, like the Hudson, had been developed from the Lockheed 18 civil airliner – and from them dropped paratroops of the Japanese 1st Raiding Group, which quickly captured the airfield. Another force of paratroops seized the nearby oil refinery after fierce fighting.

From now on, the Allies had to operate from the PII airstrip, and it was from here that reconnaissance aircraft detected a Japanese naval force *en route* to occupy the Sumatra. The convoy was attacked by every available bomber that could be mustered by the RAF and RAAF. They enjoyed a conspicuous success by sinking six enemy transports for the loss of seven aircraft, and the next day, escorted this time by Hurricanes, they attacked the enemy landing force again, inflicting enormous destruction on the landing ships in the Banka Strait and the mouth of the Palembang river. The enemy's landing plan was completely dislocated, and thousands of troops killed. In addition, the Hurricanes destroyed a number of Zero fighters on the ground at Banka Island. Unfortunately, no Allied troops or naval forces were available to exploit this success, and the position in Sumatra quickly became untenable. With stocks of food, fuel and ammunition running dangerously low, the order was given for a move to Java.

The evacuation was completed on 18 February. By that time, twenty-five Hurricanes remained, of which eighteen were serviceable; these were divided between Nos. 232 and 605 Squadrons and immediately thrown into the defence of Batavia. Twenty-four more Hurricanes – Mk Is which had been diverted in crates from Singapore to Batavia – were also operated by the Royal Netherlands Indies Army Air Corps, one for the defence of Batavia and the other for ground attack. At that time twenty-four more Hurricanes were still in crates at Batavia; these had been destined for the RAF, but as there were simply not enough pilots to fly them it was decided to turn them over to the Dutch too, along with some forty airmen and an engineering officer.

No spares, ammunition or supplies of any kind were

included and no training was offered. At the handing-over ceremony the Dutch colonel receiving the aircraft, not understanding the safety ring on the firing button, enlivened the proceedings by firing a long burst just over the heads of RAF VIPs in the parade. This set the scene for a remarkable do-it-yourself private air force, which survived for several weeks and gave the Japanese a bad time, although at great cost.

The Hurricanes and personnel moved to an improvised grass airfield north of Bandoeng in central Java, the officers and men living in grass huts in the local village. The squadron CO was Lieutenant-Colonel Animaat, a saturnine individual of demonic courage. He had little to lose, for his family had been wiped out a few weeks earlier during the Japanese invasion of the Celebes Islands, between Borneo and New Guinea. He came from Dutch Guiana, in South America, and was of very mixed blood. He was also a gentleman of the old school and spoke perfect English. His second-in-command was Captain Bruning, who had fought in the Battle of Britain and who now acted as training and conversion officer. He, too, spoke perfect English and never hid from his British colleagues his assessment of how hopeless the situation was; at the same time, he did a remarkable job of building the pilots' morale even higher. As their experience had been confined to the Curtiss Mohawk (Hawk 75A) and the even earlier Curtiss-Wright CW-21, the Hurricane was an eye-opener for them and they revelled in its speed, rate of climb and, above all, its armament and toughness.

'We are working about twenty hours a day,' the RAF

engineer officer wrote in his diary, 'cutting out dispersal pens in the rubber plantations around the airstrip, getting the locals to dig trenches, checking out the assembly work, stripping the aircraft down, teaching the Dutch pilots to handle liquid-cooled engines and constant-speed props and, above all – vital to morale, it seemed – painting the yellow triangle insignia of the Royal Netherlands Indies Army Air Corps on the aircraft.

'The Hurricanes' first operation was a total success, because eight of them – all we could get into the air – caught a formation of Japanese Navy single-engined carrier aircraft returning unescorted after a maximum-range trip and shot the lot down. That was their only easy one; after that it was nearly always fighter to fighter. We were lucky to get five minutes' warning of a raid coming in, so we were usually at a disadvantage.

'The Dutch were, however, brilliant pilots, having had years of training in the peacetime Netherlands East Indies, and the strength of the Hurricane allowed them to take ridiculous liberties with it. Some of our repairs were ridiculous, too, including using the village bicycle repairer, a Chinese, to fix damage to the fuselage trusses and the Javanese ladies to provide patches for fabric repair.

'Inevitably, we irritated the Japanese too much and they located our airfield, which was cutting up badly, and mounted a major low-level bombing and strafing attack just after our morning patrol had come in. Six aircraft were refuelling, and all were destroyed when the petrol bowsers brewed up. About fifteen of my men were killed or seriously wounded, as were several Dutch pilots. My life was saved by Bruning, who pushed me into a slit trench and fell on top of me just as another strafing wave came in.

'Our dispersed aircraft were not hit, however, and we managed to get six out of eight serviceable. The Dutch played cards to decide who was first in the queue to fly. A few days after the major raid, with even petrol almost unobtainable, Animaat was ordered to move to Soerabaya in east Java, which had been flattened and was expected to be invaded. It was obviously to be last stand and he absolutely refused to take me with him, saying that they would probably manage only one take-off and that his own ground crew of about ten men could look after that. We were returned to Bandoeng, already in chaos; some of us were ordered to evacuate and some to stay. I was lucky . . .'

Disaster in the air was quickly followed by disaster at sea. After the sinking of the *Prince of Wales* and *Repulse* off Malaya, with its incalculable consequences on the morale of the defenders of the peninsula and Singapore, had come the news on Christmas Day that Hong Kong had also fallen, with the loss to the Royal Navy of the destroyer *Thracian*, a minelayer, four gunboats and eight MTBs. Meanwhile, command of the British Eastern Fleet had been assumed by Admiral Sir Geoffrey Layton – or rather re-assumed, for he had just handed it over to the unfortunate Admiral Tom Phillips, lost with the *Prince of Wales*. It was a command with precious few ships, and a new Allied naval command called ABDA – American,

British, Dutch, Australian – set up on Java in January 1942 under Admiral T.C. Hart of the United States Navy, was scarcely in better shape.

For five weeks in January and early February, Hart's motley collection of warships – mostly British and Dutch – were employed in escorting troop convoys to Singapore, but by the end of January the Singapore naval base was so badly damaged that it could barely function. What had become the barest trickle of reinforcements was finally stopped after the Japanese gained a foothold on Singapore island on 9 February 1942, and on the twelfth, three days before the Singapore garrison surrendered, there was a mass exodus of every seaworthy vessel from the base, laden with civilian and military personnel.

On 13 February a Japanese invasion force was reported to be heading for Sumatra and the ABDA Command despatched a naval force of five cruisers and ten destroyers, including the British cruiser *Exeter*, to intercept it. However, the Allied ships were heavily attacked from the air, and although none was lost to air attack the force commander, the Dutch Admiral Karel Doorman, decided to call off the operation and withdraw.

The enemy blows now fell thick and fast. On 18 February Japanese forces landed on the island of Bali, isolating Java from the east, and on the following day aircraft of their main striking force, the 1st Carrier Air Fleet, launched a devastating attack on Port Darwin, sinking eleven transports and supply ships and causing severe damage to the port installations. As Darwin was the only base in North Australia from which Java could be reinforced and supplied, this attack effectively sealed the fate of the defenders.

On 27 February, Admiral Doorman, who had meanwhile been in action against the Japanese in the Bandoeng Strait with a mixed force of Dutch and American warships, sailed from Soerabaya with five cruisers, including the *Exeter*, and nine destroyers – three of them British – to intercept Japanese invasion forces in the Java Sea. The Japanese force was escorted by four cruisers and fourteen destroyers, and at 1600 hours the opposing cruisers began an exchange of gunfire. Shortly afterwards the *Exeter* was hit by a heavy shell and compelled to withdraw to Soerabaya escorted by the Dutch destroyer *Witte de With*, another Dutch destroyer, the *Kortenaer*, having been sunk by a torpedo. Of the 120 torpedoes launched by enemy destroyers during this phase of the battle, it was the only one that found a target. To cover the *Exeter*'s withdrawal the three British destroyers became engaged in a short-range action with eight enemy destroyers accompanying the cruiser *Naka*, and in a confused battle in poor visibility, caused by dense smoke screens, the British destroyer HMS *Electra* made a gallant single-handed attack on the enemy. She vanished into the smoke, and was seen no more.

Admiral Doorman then reformed his force with four cruisers and six destroyers and made a sortie to the north-west, where his ships fought a brief action in the dark with the cruisers *Haguro* and *Nachi*. Soon after this, the British destroyer *Jupiter* blew up – either as the result of striking a Dutch mine, or because she was torpedoed in error by the American submarine S38. The

Allied force suffered further losses during the night when the Dutch cruisers *Java* and *De Ruyter* were sunk by torpedoes; the two remaining cruisers, the USS *Houston* and HMAS *Perth*, headed for Batavia in a bid to escape from the trap that was rapidly closing on them. The four American destroyers, meanwhile, had returned to Soerabaya to re-arm and refuel, while the sole remaining British destroyer, the *Encounter*, had been despatched to pick up survivors from the *Kortenaer*.

Early in the morning of 28 February the four US destroyers passed through the Bali Strait bound for Australia, which they reached after a short and indecisive engagement with three Japanese warships. In the afternoon, the cruisers *Houston* and *Perth*, followed by the Dutch destroyer *Evertsen*, sailed from Batavia and headed into the Sunda Straits, making for Tjilatjap. During the night the two cruisers encountered another enemy invasion force and attacked it, braving formidable odds. Both cruisers were sunk by the covering force, but not before they had destroyed two transports and damaged three destroyers and a minesweeper. The *Evertsen*, coming up behind, was shelled and set on fire; her crew managed to beach her.

HMS *Exeter*, meanwhile, had sailed from Soerabaya at dusk, also heading for the Sunda Strait, accompanied by the destroyers HMS *Encounter* and USS *Pope*. On the morning of 1 March, trapped between two enemy forces, *Exeter* and *Encounter* were sunk by a combination of gunfire and torpedoes; the Pope was disabled by dive-bombers from the Japanese carrier *Ryujo* and subsequently sunk by shellfire. Some 800 survivors from the three ships were picked up by the Japanese, many to die miserably in captivity.

So ended the Battle of the Java Sea, and with it any hope of contesting the Japanese invasion of south-east Asia. The Royal Navy's assets in the theatre were effectively reduced to the old light cruisers *Danae* and *Dragon* and the destroyers *Scout* and *Tenedos*, which, accompanied by the Australian cruiser HMAS *Hobart*, had set out from the Sunda Strait for Colombo on 28 February, picking up refugees *en route*. Another British destroyer, HMS *Stronghold*, was sunk by enemy warships on 2 March during the withdrawal from Java, together with HMAS *Yarra*.

The tide of Japanese conquest swept on. Twenty-four hours after the invasion of Malaya the Japanese had landed on the island of Luzon, in the Philippines, their major assault – in which between 80,000 and 100,000 men went ashore – coming on 22 December 1941. It was preceded by violent attacks from the air, in which the capital, Manila, and the nearby naval base at Cavite were savagely bombed. American resistance was fierce, particularly on the islands of Bataan and Corregidor, but it was a hopeless battle.

In Burma, the Allies fought on.

Eight

The Sittang River, Late February 1942

The Japanese had crossed the Salween – the broad river on whose banks some Allied commanders had believed the enemy could be stopped with relative ease – and was now racing for the Sittang, only seventy miles from Rangoon. Major-General John Smyth, VC, commanding the British 17th Division, which had borne the brunt of the fighting, knew that there was only one sensible course of action, and that was to carry out a strategic retreat north to a position where he could concentrate his forces and organise a creditable defence. He summoned his old friend Brigadier 'Punch' Cowan, recently arrived at the battlefront from India, and briefed him for an urgent mission to Army Headquarters in Rangoon.

"We must get back to the Sittang, Punch," Smyth said, "and we must start now. As you are aware, the road between here and the iron railway bridge that spans the river is nothing more than a track, and it's feet deep in dust. Movement will be slow, and if we delay for too long there's every chance the enemy will out-flank us, get behind us and cut us off. I'm having the railway bridge planked to form a roadway, and I am sending back whatever troops we can spare to protect it against unforeseen attack. I've also instructed the sappers to prepare it for demolition."

He bent over a map, his finger describing a circle around the area in the vicinity of the Sittang bridge.

"You see here – on the west bank of the Sittang the country is open, and quite suitable for the type of operation for which our troops have been trained. I want to fight on grounds of my own choosing, rather than try to hold widely separated localities in thick jungle country where all the advantages lie with the Japanese. We both know what comes of holding on in impossible situations."

Cowan nodded, knowing that Smyth was referring to the last stand at Moulmein a few weeks earlier, where a British brigade had escaped by a miracle on a river steamer across the Gulf of Martaban. They had held on for two days of bitter fighting, but had lost 600 men and a great deal of equipment in the process.

"Ever since the Japanese captured Martaban they have been infiltrating between the extended, isolated positions we were ordered to hold," Smyth went on. "I'd like you to go and see the army commander, General Hutton, and explain the situation to him. What it amounts to is that our forces are being defeated because they're scattered about in penny packets. Impress upon him the grave danger in which the Division stands of being cut off from the Sittang bridge. Urge that we might be allowed to withdraw the Division behind the Bilin river immediately, where we can consolidate, and also urge that there must be no delay in the next stage of the withdrawal, which should be behind the Sittang river."

Smyth paused, studied the map intently, then said:

"I want us to get across that river well before the Japanese have a chance to intercept us. Then we shall have the support of the brigade of light tanks which is in the process of arriving. We can do it, Punch. But we must get moving right away."

A few hours later, the army commander's response came from HQ in Rangoon. The Division was to hold on. There must be no retreat. More than that: the 17th Division was to counter-attack.

It was madness. Smyth knew it, and so did Cowan. But the latter also knew the pressure to which Hutton had been subjected by General Wavell. When he returned from Rangoon, he brought with him the text of a telegram which Wavell had sent to his subordinate. It read:

"I have every confidence in judgement and fighting spirit of you and Smyth, but bear in mind that continual withdrawal, as experience of Malaya showed, is most damaging to morale of troops, especially Indian troops. Time can often be gained as effectively and less expensively, by bold counter-offensive. This especially so against Japanese."

Once again, Wavell was showing his ill-founded contempt for the Japanese soldier. It was to cost many lives, in the days to come.

The 17th Division fought valiantly, surrendering no ground to the Japanese; but as the pressure increased, every single reserve had to be thrown into the battle, and even then strong parties of enemy troops succeeded in working their way round the Division's flanks.

At last, on 19 February, the army commander gave General Smyth permission to withdraw across the Sittang. Orders were issued for the troops to break contact with the enemy under cover of darkness – a difficult enough task in itself, with only a few hundred yards separating the opposing forces.

Many of the troops, reeling with exhaustion, would never clearly remember the ordeal of that thirty-mile march to the Sittang. Bone-weary, tormented by thirst, heat and mosquitoes, there could be no rest for them. All through the night, and the following day, and the night after that, they kept going. And with the daylight came the Japanese bombers and fighters, roving back and forth along the trail at will, bombing and strafing, unmolested by any Allied aircraft.

The brigades leap-frogged back through one another, fighting rearguard actions as they did so, and by the morning of 21 February they were well clear of their pursuers, the Japanese 33rd Division. But worrying reports were reaching General Smyth that Japanese forces were out-flanking the retreating troops.

Smyth did not know, yet, that two Japanese infantry regiments had already done so, and were moving with all possible speed over cross-country tracks to intercept his Division at Sittang. It was only when his advanced headquarters came under attack by an enemy raiding force before dawn on the twenty-first that he had an inkling of how perilous the situation really was. The attack was contained, and the Japanese withdrew at daybreak.

The sun that climbed remorselessly into the Burmese sky that morning was merciless in its intensity. Its furnace-like heat was dry, adding to the torment of thirsty men and pack animals. Clouds of thick, choking red dust, kicked up by feet, hooves and wheels, hung over the trail. The dust rose for hundreds of feet, providing a constant marker for the bombers and fighters that homed in on the desperate columns. Vehicles, including ambulances crammed with wounded men, careered off the track, many to be ditched or destroyed; mules, maddened with pain where bullets or bomb fragments had struck them, or crazed by the noise, broke loose and vanished into the jungle with their loads of precious equipment, never to be seen again. Men died in their dozens and were hastily buried in makeshift graves, scooped out beside the trail.

Not all the bombs were destined for the fleeing columns. The airfield at Mingaladon lay in ruins, having been subjected to two fierce air attacks in the course of that morning. Five Hurricanes and six P-40s remained intact and airworthy. All the remaining Blenheims had been destroyed.

Armstrong was in the control tent, which had somehow survived the attacks. Landline communications with Army HQ in Rangoon had been disrupted and he was engaged in a heated conversation, not yet quite a shouting match, with an army major who had been sent out to liaise with him.

"Take a look around you, man!" Armstrong snapped, waving an arm in the general direction of what remained of the airfield. "I've got eleven fighters left, and no bombers. The ammo dump has been destroyed. The only fuel left is what's in the aircraft tanks. Of course I'd like to help the Army, but what the hell can I do? It's reinforcements I need, and equipment. They've been promised for the past week, and there's still no sign of 'em."

The major's shoulders slumped. "I know, I know," he said wearily. "I just hope to God they get here in time. The troops are just about at the end of their rope, and I don't think they'll be able to hold on at the Sittang without air support. And if the Japs cross the Sittang – well, it's next stop Rangoon."

Armstrong had never felt so utterly helpless. He recalled the original brief he'd been given, before he left for Burma, and felt like laughing or weeping. 'Use your squadron to inflict the maximum damage on the enemy, his superiors had told him. Establish airstrips behind enemy lines whenever possible. These can be stocked with fuel and supplies for ongoing operations should the enemy meet with initial success. This type of work, which you pioneered, worked well in North Africa.'

But this was not North Africa. He had no idea where the enemy lines were, except that they changed every day, and seemed to be heading in his direction. And as for fuel and supplies . . .

"We really need the Chinese to lend a hand," the major said, "but there's a diplomatic problem, apparently. The Chinese supremo, Chiang, offered General Wavell two armies, but he would only accept one division, and that's not in action yet. It's still up north in the Shan States. The

Chinese are dreadfully offended that he wouldn't accept the whole lot. After all, they've been fighting the Japs for years. The problem is, though, that the Chinese supply system is very poor. They like to live off the land wherever possible, which doesn't exactly endear them to the natives. And some of the natives in Burma, as we well know, aren't all that keen on us."

Armstrong nodded. Some time earlier, he had learned to his surprise from Donahue, the war correspondent, that pro-Japanese Burmese were fighting alongside the enemy, and that nationalist politicians, together with some Buddhist priests, were actively hostile to the British. On the other side of the coin, many Burmese Army units continued to fight hard alongside their British and Indian allies, although as the Japanese advance gathered momentum, desertion was becoming an increasing problem.

There was a sudden call from 'Sticky' Glew, who as usual had been monitoring his radio set.

"Aircraft inbound from the north," he said. "Signal is a bit fragmented, but definitely ours. ETA five minutes."

The major looked at Armstrong. "Reinforcements?" he queried hopefully.

Armstrong grunted. "I doubt it, but we can always live in hope. Let's take a look."

They went outside and peered into the northern sky through the smoke that drifted across the airfield. Flight Sergeant Cairns's valiant band of airmen were doing their best to fill in some of the bomb craters in order to create some semblance of a serviceable runway. There were no troops available to help with the task any more, and the Burmese labour force had long since disappeared.

"There they are," Armstrong said, pointing at a small gaggle of black specks. He counted six in all. If this was a reinforcement, it was not a very big one. And, as the aircraft drew nearer, he was able to see that they were not the fighters he so desperately needed. There was no mistaking the high-mounted wings, looking rather like a gull's, and the fixed undercarriage with its bulky wheel spats. The major, who had served with the British Expeditionary Force in France in 1940, recognised them too.

"Good Lord," he said. "They're Lysanders, aren't they?"

"They are indeed," Armstrong commented grimly, remembering how the RAF's Lysander squadrons had been decimated in France and North Africa. An Army co-operation aircraft, the Westland Lysander could carry six small bombs on racks attached to the wheel fairings, but the only other armament it carried was a single machine gun in the rear cockpit. But it had remarkable low-speed flying characteristics, it was extremely rugged and it could land and take off in a remarkably short distance, which made it ideal for operations from small, unprepared strips close to the front line.

The Messerschmitts had made mincemeat of it. So, Armstrong thought with a sinking feeling, would the Japanese fighters.

Some airmen had been detailed off by Flight Sergeant Cairns and were marshalling the Lysanders as they landed, indicating where they were to park. As the crews climbed out, one pilot, who was clearly the leader, spoke to Cairns, who pointed towards the control tent.

The man marched briskly over and, pulling off his flying helmet, came to attention in front of Armstrong. His dark features split into a wide grin.

"Good morning, sir. Flying Officer Mukerjee, Indian Air Force, reporting for duty."

Armstrong automatically stuck out his hand. The Indian pilot's grip was firm and strong.

"Indian Air Force?" Armstrong's face showed surprise. "I didn't know you chaps were operational yet."

Armstrong had only a sketchy knowledge of the Indian Air Force, which had been formed in 1933 from a single flight equipped with old Westland Wapiti biplanes and manned by pilots trained in England at the RAF College, Cranwell.

"Oh, yes, sir," Mukerjee told him. "We have had two flights on active service on the north-west frontier since 1938. Now two squadrons have equipped with Lysanders, and the first is fully operational. I am 'A' Flight commander, sir," he said proudly. "We are ready for action."

"Well, Mukerjee, welcome aboard," Armstrong said. "You're just what we need for tactical reconnaissance. I hope you've had plenty of training."

The Indian officer nodded vigorously. "Indeed, sir. We have developed special tactics for flying over the jungle. We are not afraid of the Japanese."

Armstrong turned to the major. "Look, the phone lines are still u/s. Why don't you nip back to Army HQ and tell your bosses that we now have reconnaissance facilities.

Ask someone to give Magwe a call and tell them to get a fuel bowser and an ammunition truck down to us, fast."

Magwe was the airfield to the north. His surplus pilots had already been sent back there; it was senseless to keep them at Mingaladon when they no longer had aircraft to fly. It had not yet been attacked by the enemy, and there were still plentiful stocks of fuel and ammunition. In the meantime, Armstrong decided that he would have fuel transferred from his damaged Hurricanes to a couple of the Lysanders, so that they would be ready to fly reconnaissance sorties in the afternoon. At least Army HQ would then be able to form a clearer picture of the situation at Sittang.

The situation, in fact, was becoming increasingly desperate in the confused and bitter fighting that took place on the road to the bridge. There were many acts of heroism, many tragedies. At one spot, a British officer commanding a company of Gurkhas was astonished to come upon a dozen dejected-looking Japanese soldiers, all of whom raised their hands. He stepped forward to accept their surrender, knowing that no Japanese prisoners had yet been taken and that some were badly needed for interrogation.

He had only gone a few yards when the Japanese threw themselves flat and a concealed machine gun behind them opened up, killing the officer and three of his men. The other Gurkhas swept forward and overwhelmed the Japanese, killing them all.

The Gurkhas would never again even consider taking Japanese prisoners.

The fate of the tiny, embattled Anglo-Indian army in Burma depended on that single bridge over the deep, swift-flowing Sittang river. It had eleven spans, each a 150 feet long. Planks placed over the rails provided a makeshift road for vehicles to cross, and this movement began at two o'clock in the morning of 22 February.

Two hours later, a truck skidded off the planks and jammed itself in the girders. It took two hours of exhausting effort before it could be moved – two hours during which no more vehicles could cross the bridge; two hours in which the Japanese spearheads moved inexorably closer.

On the east bank of the Sittang, the Allied bridgehead was defended by seven battalions of infantry and three artillery batteries, which were running out of ammunition and short of mules to pull their guns. The Japanese pressure was now intense, and preparations to blow the bridge were completed by 1800 hours on the twenty-second. All General Smyth could hope to do now was to rush as many men and as much equipment as possible across the bridge during the night, and then give the order for it to be destroyed at the very last moment. He had another factor to consider, too: the possibility that the Japanese might attempt to land airborne forces behind him.

At 0330 hours in the morning of 23 February there was a sudden burst of firing from the jungle east of the bridge, and the bridgehead troops were soon under heavy attack by the leading elements of the two Japanese regiments that had been sent around the flanks through the jungle to intercept the retreating 17th Division. The first onrush penetrated almost to the bridge itself, but was held by a battalion of the Frontier Force Regiment and a company of the Duke of Wellington's, the latter having arrived only a day earlier. A counter-attack by a Gurkha battalion threw the enemy back.

There were still thousands of men on the eastern bank of the Sittang, and a strong force of Japanese troops – growing even stronger by the hour – now lay between them and the bridge. It was strong enough, after a furious battle, to throw back two Gurkha battalions which were attempting to break through.

All that day a fierce close-quarter battle raged on the east bank. It degenerated into a jungle dogfight in which the brigades and battalions became broken up into small groups. The bridgehead defences were once again nearly overwhelmed, but the British and Indian troops put up a magnificent fight and the Japanese were again bloodily repulsed.

Towards nightfall the fighting died down and General Smyth, utterly exhausted after two days and nights of battle, went to his Divisional HQ to snatch some sleep, leaving Brigadiers Cowan and Noel Hugh-Jones, the latter commanding the all-Gurkha 48th Brigade, to supervise the evacuation from the east bank.

"At all costs," Smyth emphasised, "the bridge must not be allowed to fall into Japanese hands."

The demolition charges were in position, and the sappers were standing by. The bridge itself was now within range of the enemy's machine guns. Hugh-Jones knew that it would take only one big assault to capture it. Unwilling to make the decision that would consign thousands of men on the far bank to their doom, he consulted Cowan. Should the bridge be blown without further delay?

But there was only one man who could, in all reality, make the fateful decision. At 0430 hours, Cowan woke General Smyth and asked him to speak to Hugh-Jones. The latter told him that he could not guarantee to hold the bridge for more than another hour, and requested permission to blow it.

Smyth consulted with his own conscience. He had to make a horrible decision. If the bridge was blown, two-thirds of his Division would be trapped on the far bank. If he did not give the order to blow it, two Japanese divisions could march straight on to Rangoon.

The decision was his, and his alone. It took him less than five minutes to make up his mind. The bridge was to be blown immediately.

The troops in comparative safety on the west bank did what they could to help their less fortunate comrades, firing tracers into the air at minute intervals, flashing lamps, blowing whistles, even singing to help the men on the other side to find the bridge in the darkness. Then, at 0530 hours, as the sappers withdrew under the cover of machine guns manned by officers, three mighty explosions shattered the night.

On both sides the firing ceased, and a strange silence hung over the battlefield. It lasted several minutes, and was broken by the Japanese, who began to shout and chatter excitedly.

All along the east bank of the river, troops who had managed to break through the Japanese cordon heard the explosions with horror, for they knew what they signified. They had been abandoned by their army.

Yet in the minds of many, there was no thought of defeat, or surrender. A few managed to get across the river, still bearing their weapons, on improvised bamboo rafts or by clinging to empty petrol tins lashed together with puttees; others had no alternative but to abandon their weapons and equipment and swim for it. Many drowned; others were shot by the enemy as they tried to cross.

Exhausted and famished, many of them naked, the survivors were sent to Wau, eight miles back from the river, where there was a railhead, and from there to Pegu, where they were re-clothed.

As many as 8,500 officers and men – British, Indians, Gurkhas – of the 17th Division had been killed, wounded or captured; 3,500 had escaped.

For the time being, the 17th Division had ceased to exist as an effective fighting force. And in the next forty-eight hours, as the Japanese hurriedly constructed temporary bridges over the Sittang and prepared to advance on Rangoon, the full fury of their air force was again turned on the Burmese capital.

Nine

The Japanese were on the move again. Their engineers had thrown pontoon bridges across the Sittang and the spearhead troops were already across, forging along the road taken by the remnants of a 17th Division a couple of days earlier – the road that led to Pegu and Rangoon.

At the controls of the Lysander, Flying Officer Mukerjee gave every impression of a man enjoying himself. The aircraft flitted like a huge green moth in and out of gullies and ravines and around jungle slopes, dropping down to ground level to investigate tracks and stretches of road.

The Indian pilot had not been joking when he had mentioned that the Lysander squadron had developed special flying techniques for reconnaissance flights over the jungle. It was hair-raising stuff, but it worked. In several days of operations over the front line, the Lysanders had often been shot at, but so far none had been lost.

In the adjacent seat, Stanislaw Kalinski made pencil marks on the map that lay folded on his knee, carefully logging the position of each Japanese unit that was sighted. An army column on the move made a lot of noise, and in almost every case the Lysander was right on top of the motorised infantry before they spotted it. While the gunner gave the enemy soldiers a burst to distract them, Kalinski made an estimate of the unit's size and composition, noted its location, and within seconds Mukerjee was twisting out of danger across the treetops. It was a comforting thought that the green-camouflaged Lysander, although quite a large aircraft, was virtually impossible to spot against the jungle backdrop by the pilots of any fighters that might be patrolling at higher altitude.

"All right," Kalinski said. "Let's go home." An experienced army co-operation pilot himself – he had flown observation aircraft during his time with the French Air Force after escaping from Nazi-occupied Poland – he was full of admiration for the Indian pilot's skill.

Half an hour later, as they walked away from the Lysander after landing at Mingaladon, Kalinski had a sudden thought. Turning to his companion, he said:

"I say, old chap, what's your first name?"

"M.O.," the Indian officer said cheerfully, possibly misunderstanding the question. "It is M.O. Mukerjee, sir."

Kalinski grinned. "Okay, then. 'Mo' it is." And Mo it was, thereafter.

It was the first day of March, and the previous month had ended with a spurt of considerable activity. Thanks to the belated arrival of fuel and ammunition from the base at Magwe, the few remaining Hurricanes and P-40s had been able to resume operational flying.

Armstrong, whose neck continued to bother him, was still unfit for combat flying, so Bob Neale, the American, had taken charge of what was left of the Mingaladon Wing, with Dickie Baird as his number two. On 25 February, as luck would have it, Neale's half-dozen P-40s were taking their turn at readiness when they were 'scrambled' to intercept Japanese bombers approaching Rangoon. There were forty of them, escorted by twenty Zero fighters, but for once the defenders had received plenty of warning.

When the Japanese formation arrived, Neale and his five pilots were poised up-sun, in an ideal position to intercept. In the short, whirlwind air battle that followed, Neale personally destroyed four bombers and probably destroyed another; his pilots claimed another six enemy aircraft between them.

Kalinski found Armstrong in conference with Neale, Baird and the major from Army HQ. The Pole handed his marked map to the latter, who studied it carefully.

"They'll be flooding over the river soon," he remarked grimly. "We've got to do our utmost to slow them down. Lord! I feel like the little Dutch kid who stuck his finger in the hole in the dyke to stop the water coming through."

"Army HQ want us to attack the pontoons," Armstrong explained, looking at Kalinski. "Or rather, they'll be attacked by a force of Blenheims now being assembled at Magwe. Flight Lieutenant Craig will be leading them. We'll be providing top cover. It won't be a picnic. We know the Japs have some Zeros in the area, and they're better than anything else they've got. We've got eleven serviceable fighters between us and we'll have to use all of them, which will mean leaving Rangoon undefended, but it can't be helped. The Blenheims will need all the help we can give them."

Mukerjee, who had been listening intently, suddenly stepped forward.

"Sir, I have a suggestion. My Lysanders can carry bombs. Not very large bombs, but bombs nonetheless. May we be permitted to take part in this attack?"

Armstrong sucked on his pipe, his brow furrowed. Mukerjee spoke up again.

"I know there will be a great risk, sir, but if we time our attack carefully I think we can get away with it. The enemy defences will have eyes only for the Blenheims. They will not be looking for aircraft coming in from a different direction, at low level. We will be exposed to fire for only a minute, perhaps two at the most. Please let us try."

"It's worth a shot, Ken," Neale said. "And we've got some two-hundred-and-fifty-pounders. Salvaged 'em from the docks the other day, if you remember."

Armstrong pondered for a moment longer, then nodded. "All right, then. It will take some fine tuning, though. Let's get down to details."

In Rangoon, the Army Commander, General Hutton, was also getting down to details. Few commanders in the history of warfare could have been faced with more problems than Hutton, who had laboured under a series of crippling handicaps ever since he had assumed command at the time of the Japanese invasion. It was to his credit that, working tirelessly, he had managed to get many essential stores moved out of the capital and distributed to other centres in Burma – the more so since he was a far from fit man, having been involved in a serious air crash, in which his pilot was killed, only a couple of months earlier.

Faced with the inevitable, Hutton and his staff now laid final plans for the demolition of the docks, oil storage tanks and other vital installations in Rangoon. By this time, law and order in the capital had broken down almost completely. All the public services had ceased to function. There was no water or electricity, and no sanitation service to clear the streets of refuse and corpses.

The roads around Rangoon were choked with refugees, mostly Indians. One tide headed north, trekking towards the Indian border; another poured into the city, fleeing from the countryside and hoping to escape by ship. These poor people had to contend not only with starvation and disease, but with attacks by Dacoits and hostile Burmese, who raped, robbed and murdered at will. No one even bothered to glance any more at the corpses that drifted down the river; no one paid any attention to the looting and mayhem that reigned after darkness fell on Rangoon's streets.

Desperate men, women and children tried to scramble aboard any ship that might take them to safety. Troops with fixed bayonets held them back. Those that did manage to board some vessel any vessel – and tried to hide on it were rooted out and flung into the river. Orders were orders.

European women and children had already been evacuated north to Mandalay, from where, after resting, they went on to Calcutta. One of the last vehicles to leave was driven by an elderly lady whose companion, no longer having any tea and sandwiches to dispense, sat in the back of the Salvation Army van and tried to keep its load of terrified children happy by singing to them.

Other magnificent women flatly refused to be evacuated and continued to carry out their vital tasks. In Mingaladon hospital, Sister Philippa Windrush and her small staff, reduced now to half a dozen, continued their ministrations to a handful of badly wounded patients who were too ill to be moved. The nurses gave no sign of the terror they felt, the dread of what would almost certainly happen to them if they fell into Japanese hands.

At two o'clock that afternoon, Philippa Windrush, dog-tired after having been on duty for nearly twenty-four hours, went out on to the veranda, sat down, drank half a cup of tea and immediately fell asleep. Her nap lasted only a few minutes before she was jerked awake by the roar of aero-engines.

Looking up, experiencing a sudden snap of panic in case the aircraft were Japanese raiders, she felt relief as she recognised them to be familiar shapes, machines from the nearby airfield. There were six of them, those ungainly-looking aircraft with the gull-like wings she had first noticed a few days ago. Flying at low altitude, they dwindled rapidly into the eastern sky.

A few minutes later others came, fighters this time, climbing hard and fast. They would soon overtake the aircraft in front, she thought, and wondered where they were going. There seemed to be so few of them. She thought of the pilot she had met a while back, the one who had been injured when his plane came down in the water, and felt disappointed that he had not been in touch with her since he left hospital. Then she shook her head in irritation at herself.

Why should he feel the need to contact her? she asked herself. He was a senior officer, a wing commander, doubtless with a thousand and one things to do each day. He probably hadn't even given her a passing thought.

She looked at the specks that were now barely visible in the east. What if he were up there, in one of those planes, perhaps heading into danger? What if something had already happened to him?

Sister Philippa Windrush suddenly realised that she was thinking the thoughts of a moonstruck adolescent. She decided that a cold bath would do the trick. She got up, looking eastwards, but the aircraft were out of sight.

She could not know that the aircraft she had just seen were not the only ones heading for what might be a fatal rendezvous. Some time earlier, eight Bristol Blenheim bombers had taken off from Magwe, 200 miles north of Mingaladon, and were now heading south-south-east. From the pilot's seat of the leading aircraft, Roger Craig peered ahead through the Perspex nose; so did his observer-bomb aimer, an Australian lad who looked too young even to be allowed anywhere near an aeroplane, let alone navigate it and drop bombs from it.

After a while they found what they were both looking for: the shimmering ribbon of the Sittang river. As it disappeared under the nose of his aircraft Craig initiated a gentle right-hand turn, followed by the rest of the formation, so that they were on a southerly heading towards their target. The altimeter showed 8,000 feet.

Twenty miles ahead, and 7,000 feet higher up, the fighter escort had already reached the target area. The fighters circled, well out of range of light anti-aircraft fire, the P-40s in the lead and the Hurricanes bringing up the rear. Baird was leading the five Hurricanes; the other pilots were Kalinski, O'Day and two New Zealand flying officers, McKenzie and Robinson, both of whom had flown Brewster Buffaloes before converting to the Hurricane.

All eyes were on the sun, the dangerous sun where the Zeros might be lurking. He suspected that the Jap fighters were even now gaining height somewhere over Siam, and that once they had the advantage of altitude and sun they would come down hard and fast, seeking to break up the Allied fighters and then attacking individual aircraft.

Baird's surmise was quite correct. At that moment, a dozen Zeros were climbing hard and fast, their pilots already aware – thanks to a network of agents in Burma – that bombers had taken off from Magwe and were heading for the battlefront. The fighter leader, Lieutenant Toru Saito, knew that the Sittang pontoon bridges were the most likely target.

The Zero, properly called Mitsubishi A6M Type 0, quivered like a thoroughbred under Saito's light touch. It was a splendid fighter, and a delight to fly. It would climb to 10,000 feet in three minutes flat at a steady angle of forty-five degrees under the power of its 1,300 horsepower Nakajima Sakai radial engine, which was a development of the French Gnome-Rhone, and it could reach a speed of 350 miles per hour.

Some pilots joked that the Zero was little more than a lightweight sporting aircraft fitted with a powerful engine, but there was more than just an element of truth in that. The fighter's secret lay in the way in which Mitsubishi's designers had planned its construction. Instead of being built in separate units – wings, fuselage, tail unit and so on – the Zero was constructed in two pieces. The engine, cockpit and forward part of the fuselage combined with the wings to form a single rigid unit; the second unit consisted of the rear part of the fuselage and the tail. The two parts were held together by a ring of eighty bolts.

The whole aircraft weighed less than 4,000 pounds. It was half a ton lighter than the Hurricane. It also packed a powerful punch: two twenty-millimetre cannons in the wings and a pair of machine guns in the nose.

Operating from an airfield was something of a novelty for Saito and his pilots, for the squadron belonged to the Imperial Japanese Navy and normally flew from an aircraft carrier. In fact, it had been operating from the carrier *Ryujo* in support of the invasion of Java when it had been temporarily deployed to Siam in response to an urgent request from the Japanese Army Commander in Burma, General Sakurai, whose troops needed additional air cover for the drive on Rangoon.

The pilots were now within sight of the Sittang and one of them, with keener eyes than the others, spotted the Allied fighters circling over the bridges and called a warning over the radio. But it was Saito himself who was the first to see the formation of Blenheims, skimming a few thousand feet above the relatively flat terrain immediately to the north. Brusquely, he ordered the squadron to split up. Six pilots were to engage the bombers while the other six, led by himself, would take on the fighters.

Saito's half-dozen plummeting Zeros were not seen by the British and American pilots until it was almost too late. There was not even time to make a proper R/T call; one of the New Zealanders, McKenzie, shouted "Look out, bandits!" an instant before he was shot down by Saito. His Hurricane went into the ground vertically and exploded in a bubble of flame.

The remaining Hurricanes scattered in all directions and Saito dived through the middle of them. Baird, furious at being taken by surprise, flung his Hurricane after him and opened fire. His cone of bullets encountered only thin air, for at that precise moment Saito pulled his Zero up into a perfect tight loop that brought him on to Baird's tail. Baird, who had never seen anyone perform such a manoeuvre in combat, was too astonished to be frightened, but it was only a reflex action that enabled him to get away. Turning the Hurricane on its back, he pulled hard on the stick and went into a vertical dive, pulling out just above the jungle canopy. Standing the fighter on its wingtip, he came round in a turn so tight that it brought the Hurricane close to stalling, looking back as he did so.

There was no sign of his attacker. Streaming sweat, he climbed back towards the battle.

Meanwhile, Bob Neale and his AVG pilots had become aware of the danger to the incoming bombers, having seen the other six Zeros diving fast from astern. The Americans broke and split up, turning hard in the hope of getting on the Japs' tails as their high speed carried them past. A Zero flashed past Neale's nose and he got in a short deflection burst. It was a lucky shot; the burst hit the enemy fighter just behind the cockpit, in the vulnerable spot where the tail section was joined to the forward fuselage and wings, and the Zero fell to pieces, fluttering down into the jungle.

A few hundred yards away a P-40 was twisting and turning in a desperate attempt to elude a Zero, which clung to its tail and fired in short, accurate bursts. Neale closed in on the enemy fighter, whose pilot had not seen him, and opened fire when the Zero filled his sights. The Japanese fighter streamed white smoke and disintegrated. It was all over in two seconds, but the action was too late to save the P-40. Three more Zeros had latched on to it and the American pilot, knowing that he could not out-run them – he had insufficient height to gain speed by means of a dive – went into a tight turn through 360 degrees, a manoeuvre that gained a little ground.

Rolling out on a northerly heading, the American sped away, but in less than a minute the Zeros had caught up with him again and forced him into another turn. With three against one, the outcome was inevitable. Concentrating on getting away from the first Zero, the American pilot ran into a burst from the third enemy fighter, who had managed to cut across the P-40's turn.

The American fighter burst into flames and flew into a hillside.

The Japanese pilots were now concentrating some of their effort on the Blenheims, which were starting their bombing run. The pilots held doggedly to their course as their gunners tried desperately to fend off the attacks. So far, only three Zeros were involved.

The Blenheims, which had descended to 3,000 feet, made their attack singly, in line astern, aiming to drop their bombs diagonally across the pontoons. In the leading aircraft, Roger Craig saw a Zero appear off to starboard and begin to close in, only to turn away and disappear, its pilot probably scared off by the light anti-aircraft fire which was now coming up thick and fast. Craig's bomb-aimer pressed the release and four 250-pound bombs fell from the aircraft's belly. Feeling extremely vulnerable in the Blenheim's 'glasshouse' cockpit, Craig took the aircraft down to less than a hundred feet and followed the course of the river until he was well clear of the target area. Only then did he pull up a little and set course for Mingaladon, where the bombers were to refuel before returning to Magwe.

Diving to the attack astern of Craig, the pilot of the second Blenheim saw his leader's bombs erupt around the far end of one of the pontoon bridges. Levelling out at 2,000 feet, he dropped his own bombs and was disappointed when his gunner reported that they had exploded in the water and on the river bank.

Disappointment turned to alarm when the gunner reported an enemy fighter closing in astern. An instant later, the Blenheim shuddered violently as cannon shells slammed into its port wing. The gunner's fire drove off the Zero, but by now flames were streaming from a fuel tank. The pilot eased the bomber round until its nose was pointing northwards, attempting to get as close as possible to unoccupied territory before the tank exploded, and was on the point of ordering the crew to bale out when the fire suddenly went out. Almost sick with relief, he nursed the Blenheim to Mingaladon.

The third Blenheim never got as far as the bridges. Torn apart by fire from two Zeros, its crew dead or dying, it flew into the ground and its bomb load exploded, sending up a huge cloud of smoke and dust.

The fourth bomber flew through the writhing cloud, was hit almost immediately by a storm of ground fire, and burst into flames. Its pilot held on long enough to release his bombs, and despite severe burns managed to make a perfect belly landing. Taken prisoner by the Japanese, he died under interrogation. The other two crew members were also brutally interrogated, then murdered by their captors.

The fifth Blenheim, on the point of being attacked by a Zero, was saved by Kalinski, who dived down out of a mêlée higher up and opened fire on the fighter from a range of 150 yards. His bullets chewed up the Zero from nose to tail and its propeller turned more slowly until it stopped altogether. Suddenly, the outer section of a wing broke off and the Japanese fighter went into a series of flick rolls that ended abruptly when it hit the ground and blew up. In the next breath, the Polish pilot was forced to sheer away violently when the Blenheim's gunner opened fire on him.

"Bloody gratitude for you," he muttered, as he climbed to rejoin the fight above.

The sixth Blenheim made its attack, bombed accurately, and got clear of the target area without so much as a scratch. The seventh was not so lucky. Ablaze from wingtip to wingtip, it rose in a near-vertical climb as the nervous reflexes of its dead pilot jerked back the control column, then stalled and plunged to earth, where it disintegrated in the explosion of its bomb load.

The eighth Blenheim suddenly appeared off to one side of the bridges, turning steeply and shedding fragments as the flak hit it. It dived into the western end of one of the bridges in a terrific explosion as its bombs detonated.

Overhead, both sets of fighters suddenly broke contact with one another as though on a given signal and flew off in opposite directions. The Japanese anti-aircraft gunners, sweating with exertion, peered into the northern sky, saw no more incoming aircraft, and began to relax a little.

They were still looking towards the north when, with a thunderclap of sound, Mukerjee's six Lysanders appeared out of nowhere, sped over the twin bridges in impeccable line abreast, and dropped twenty-four bombs on them. When the smoke and spray cleared, the infuriated Japanese saw new gaps in the bridges, adding to the damage already inflicted by the Blenheims. The Lysanders, not one of them hit, broke formation and vanished into jungle-clad ravines.

The battle had cost the Japanese three Zeros. It had cost the Allies a Hurricane, a P-40 and half the Blenheim force.

It took the Japanese engineers less than twenty-four hours to repair the bridges. Once more, the Japanese Army began to roll towards Rangoon.

Ten

The great mushroom of smoke rose more than three miles into the sky over Rangoon. Thick and impenetrable, it roiled up from the oil refineries of the Burmah Oil Company, from fuel dumps, the dock areas, the power station, food depots and warehouses.

The demolition squads had done their work well. The destruction of all essential facilities in Rangoon was complete. From the city itself the sun was blotted out so completely that, in places, the only light came from the glare of fires. It was a terrifying, hellish vista, made all the more so by the shadowy figures who still wandered the ruined streets.

They were criminals, lunatics and lepers, released from the gaols and institutions by an official of the Indian Civil Service who had misunderstood an instruction. 5,000 convicts, most of them dangerous, prowled streets that were deserted except for a rearguard of troops armed with rifles and tommy-guns, their orders to shoot looters on sight.

The lepers and lunatics, desperate for food, descended on the city's refuse heaps, where they fought mongrel dogs for scraps. Incongruously, through the nightmare scenes, there wandered an occasional Buddhist monk, protected from assault by the saffron robes of his faith.

The Army Commander in Burma, General Hutton, had been relieved at long last. His successor was General Sir Harold Alexander, veteran of the campaigns in the Western Desert. He arrived in Rangoon only just in time to supervise the final evacuation, unaware that a trap was about to spring on the capital.

The Japanese plan was to enter Rangoon from the north-west, and to this end the 33rd Division, approaching from the east by paths through hills and jungle, by-passed the city to the north, leaving one strong road-block astride the road that led to Prome – the principal road of evacuation – to protect its flank while the movement was under way. The British troops attempting to leave Rangoon were now effectively bottled up, and although they made several strong attacks on the road-block they were unable to shift it. The British, tied as they were to their mechanical transport and a single ribbon of road, seemed doomed.

Suddenly, the road-block disappeared. The Japanese commander, sticking rigidly to his orders, had withdrawn it once the rest of the division had made the crossing to the north of Rangoon. The cork was out of the bottle. By pure chance, the destruction of the whole British force in Rangoon, and with it General Alexander and his headquarters, had been averted.

On 6 March, the few remaining aircraft at Mingaladon were flown out to Magwe. The last to leave were Mukerjee's six Lysanders, and they carried an unusual cargo: the British nursing staff from Mingaladon hospital, including a very reluctant Philippa Windrush. The Burmese staff had volunteered to stay behind to look after the few remaining wounded; nothing could be done for the latter in any case, and the Burmese could actually pretend that they welcomed the Japanese invaders.

The final evacuation of Rangoon took place on the following day. Some personnel embarked on steamers, which slipped through the Twante Canal under cover of darkness and joined the Irrawaddy; others piled on to trains, the last of which left the city at seven-thirty in the morning.

A few brave souls held out until the very last moment, causing as much damage as possible before the first Japanese arrived. One of them was Bobby McLean-Brown of the Rangoon Docks Commission, whose young family had already been evacuated. With a group of men who had remained loyal, he hastened from wharf to wharf, making sure that everything that might be of possible use to the enemy was thoroughly destroyed. River boats and sampans were scuttled, the dispositions of buoys that marked safe channels altered in the hope that Japanese ships would run aground.

McLean-Brown and his men came very close to disaster. Commandeering the only surviving tugboat, they set off along the Twante Canal, only to find their way blocked by a boatload of armed and hostile Burmese – about eighty in all, the British engineer reckoned. Increasing speed, McLean-Brown pointed the tug's bow at the other boat and sliced it neatly in two. The few Burmese who tried to board the tug were easily dealt with.

The Rising Sun

At about midday on 8 March 1942, the 215th Infantry Regiment of the Japanese 33rd Division entered Rangoon. The astonished troops, who had fully expected to meet strong resistance, instead found the streets deserted except for the lepers, criminals and the insane – and wild animals from the local zoo, which had been deliberately released.

All categories of creature found wandering the streets, human or otherwise, were destroyed with equal zeal.

The Japanese commander, General Sakurai, suddenly realised that the long convoy of vehicles his reconnaissance aircraft had seen leaving the city had contained the whole of the Anglo-Indian garrison. He ordered elements of the 33rd Division to pursue it, but it was too late.

The longest fighting retreat in the history of the British Army had begun. The sanctuary of the Indian border was 1,200 miles away.

At least the troops, for the most part, had transport; thousands of luckless civilians did not. Those without money or influence suffered terrible privations as they trekked the long road north; the Indians in particular, most of whom had worked for a pittance, were now short of almost every necessity. Constantly attacked by Burmese bandits, who robbed and butchered the leaderless caravans, they trudged on in the one blind hope that they would somehow reach India.

The caravans numbered thousands of people. They could travel only a few miles each day, as their pace was dictated by that of the plodding oxen who pulled their cumbersome carts. Each caravan completely blocked the road for up to half a mile. The refugees travelled only by night, for this shielded them from Japanese aircraft and also protected them to some extent from bandit attacks. The bandits favoured attacking resting caravans at night; their tactics were to sneak around the edges of a caravan, seeking out and killing groups who had chosen to rest away from the main body, and then plundering their pitiful possessions.

The civilian Indians of Burma were simple, gentle folk who had known only a lifetime of subservience. They looked, with pathetic pleading in their eyes, to those who had governed them for guidance and help, and found none.

The fighting Indians, and these included the Gurkhas, were a different story.

During the retreat, a small group of Hindu troops, part of a retreating column, came upon a Bhuddist monastery and asked their officer for permission to approach it more closely. Perhaps they would be able to buy or make trade for water and provisions; monasteries were often built over or near natural springs. Permission was granted, but the men were warned that the column would not wait for them. Later, when the column stopped to rest, some Gurkhas were sent back to look for the missing men.

After a while, the Gurkhas returned and reported that the Hindu soldiers had been admitted into the monastery, where they had all been murdered. Almost as an after-thought, one of the Gurkhas, whose lethal *kukri* knife stood out unsheathed in his belt, smiled at the officer and hoped that the Captain *Sahib* would not be too upset by the news that the monks were also now dead.

The town of Prome, with its bungalows, its neat lawns and gardens, had once been an attractive place. Now it was visited by Japanese bombers every other day or so, almost always at breakfast time, and fires raged everywhere, some of them started by Japanese sympathisers.

Prome was crammed with Indian refugees, many with smallpox and cholera, encamped along the streets and river wharves, waiting to cross the Irrawaddy and continue their trek towards the Arakan coast and India itself. To keep the streets clear of refuse and corpses, the authorities released criminals in batches from the local gaol and gave them their liberty in return for a few days' work as street-cleaners.

Many of the retreating troops were scarcely in better shape than the refugees. Thousands did not have the benefit of transport and had to struggle back through the jungle. All their equipment had gone, except for a haversack, a water-bottle and a sock filled with rice. Many dropped out through sheer exhaustion, malaria or dysentery. Malaria would return to haunt the survivors at intervals for the rest of their lives, a legacy of Burma. The worst dysentery cases, those still able to stagger on, threw aside their filth-caked pants and fashioned crude loincloths from strips of shirt. Almost all had jungle sores, circles of corruption the size of half-crowns that ate into the flesh like acid, down to the bone.

They were broken not by the enemy, but by the jungle and the merciless sun. Yet, amid all the chaos of retreat, all the untold misery, there were glimmers of hope.

A new senior British officer arrived in Burma. He was

appointed to command what became known as the Burma Corps – 'Burcorps' for short. This command consisted of the 1st Burma Division, the 17th Indian Division and the 7th Armoured Brigade, the latter experienced veterans of the fighting in North Africa, as well as other units.

The officer's name was General Bill Slim. His daunting, seemingly impossible task was to turn defeat into victory.

As Slim strove to regroup his forces on a defensive line between Prome and Toungoo, the former on the Irrawaddy and the latter on the Sittang, another charismatic figure arrived in Burma to take command of the Chinese armies there. He was the American General Joseph W. Stilwell. Friends, of whom he had few, and enemies, of whom he had many, alike nicknamed him 'Vinegar Joe'.

A Chinese army was an extraordinary affair. It comprised two or three divisions, each much smaller than its British counterpart. Only two thirds of the men were armed; the other third acted literally as pack animals, burdened down with rations and equipment. There were no artillery units, no medical services, a couple of staff cars for the top brass, half a dozen trucks and a couple of hundred shaggy, ill-kempt ponies.

The Chinese soldier was tough, brave and very experienced. He had been fighting the Japanese for years.

When they began to receive trucks from the Americans, the Chinese learned to drive as they went along. Chinese drivers were notorious. Trucks ranging in size from two and a half to ten tons would storm in close convoy along the roads of Burma at fifty or sixty miles per hour. The inevitable result was that if a truck up front came to grief, so did half a dozen of the ones behind it.

Passing a Chinese convoy was a hazardous business. For one thing, the clouds of choking dust it raised obscured everything ahead and on either side. For another, it kept to the middle of the road, so that anyone wishing to get past had to tear along the edge of the roadway, with the attendant risk of falling down the *bund*, as the raised embankment on which the road was built was called. By far the safest method was not to try to overtake at all, but to halt for an hour or so while the convoy got miles ahead.

Armstrong, his throat caked with dust, had decided on that very course of action. That morning, he had set off in a jeep borrowed from the American Volunteer Group to collect two replacement pilots and an intelligence officer from Mandalay. It was *en route* back to Magwe, with his passengers, that he had encountered the convoy, bound south-east towards the Sittang.

Armstrong had volunteered to make the trip for two reasons. One, he had never been to Mandalay; and two, although he was fit to fly again, he and his surviving pilots had been ordered to take a break from operations by Air Vice-Marshal Stevenson, the RAF commander in Burma. The handful of Hurricanes had been absorbed into the newly formed Burma Wing – 'Burwing' – which, based at Akyab, consisted of No. 17 Fighter Squadron and the Blenheims of No. 45, together with some AVG P-40s and the Indian Air Force Lysander Flight.

A second mixed fighter and bomber wing, 'Akwing', had been established at Akyab, on the Arakan coast.

This comprised No. 67 Squadron, with a few Hurricanes and a couple of Buffaloes, and No. 139 Squadron, with Lockheed Hudsons.

The size of the Burma Wing was decided by the maintenance resources already in Burma, for no supplies or reinforcements could reach central Burma by land or sea – except by the Burma Road from China, which was the way Armstrong's three passengers had come. All were Americans; the two pilots had been serving with the AVG squadrons at Lashio, close to the Chinese border, the Intelligence Officer had recently arrived from the United States to join General Chennault's command.

The Intelligence Officer, a captain whose name was Ignatius T. Silberman ("'Iggy' to my pals," he told Armstrong cheerfully) turned out to be a fluent Japanese linguist and an expert in most things Japanese, not least the Japanese Air Force. When Armstrong asked him how this came to be, Silberman just shook his head and shrugged.

"Dunno," he said. "They always just fascinated me, that's all. And I ain't even been there. Don't suppose I ever will, now."

As they stretched their legs by the roadside, smoking, always making sure that the tommy-guns they carried they were within easy reach – the road between Magwe and Mandalay was notorious bandit country – Silberman said that something was being done about code-names for Japanese aircraft, which Bob Sandell had suggested before his death.

"We think we've cracked the way in which the Japs

designate their airplanes," Silberman said, "but it's fantastically complicated. At the experimental stage, each prototype is allocated what they call a *Kitai* number, or 'Ki' number for short. Later, when the type goes into production, it gets a registration that includes the manufacturer's name – Mitsubishi, for example – a number indicating the year of manufacture, a description of its function, and a type number. And if you think that's complex enough, wait until I tell you that the Japanese calendar is based on the foundation of the Japanese Empire in 660 BC."

Armstrong did some mental arithmetic. "So 1939 is actually 2599 by their reckoning?"

Silberman nodded. "That's right. So an aircraft manufactured in 1937 becomes the Type Ninety-Seven, and so on. But in 1940 – year 2600 – whereas the Army Air Force used the designation 'one hundred', the Navy used only the last two digits, 00. Hence the fighter we call the Zero, which entered service in 1940, as far as we know. The trouble is, we've fallen into the habit of referring to all their fighters as Zeros, which is dangerous."

"I'll go along with that," Armstrong said, thinking of the difference in performance between the Zero and earlier Japanese fighter types. He also knew that any Japanese aircraft with more than one engine was automatically assumed to be a Mitsubishi design.

"Anyway," Silberman continued, "there's an organisation in the States called the Technical Air Intelligence Unit. I was part of it till I was shipped out here. Its director, Colonel McCoy, is keen to follow up this idea of giving code-names to Jap airplanes. He's suggested boys' names for fighters, girls' names for bombers. Zeke, Pete, Rufe and Jake are a few on his list, if I remember rightly."

"Sounds like he's from Tennessee," said one of the AVG pilots, laughing.

"You're quite right," the Intelligence Officer said. "He is."

The conversation lapsed for a while, and Armstrong's thoughts turned to Mandalay. Brought up on Rudyard Kipling's ballad, he had expected something exotic; instead he had found a dry and dusty town of tin shanties encompassed by high, thick walls, the legacy of some long-dead Burmese king. It was much knocked about by Japanese bombing. Most of the administration had moved out to Maymyo, forty miles to the north-east on a plateau of the Shan mountain range. It was the summer capital of Burma, so they said, with English-style houses and spacious gardens.

It was there that Army HQ had installed itself after its rapid exodus from Rangoon. What General Slim could not understand, when he visited Maymyo soon after his arrival, was that the Air HQ, instead of being situated alongside its Army counterpart, was hundreds of miles away in Calcutta. It was hardly an effective recipe for co-operation. It was also a situation which, in the fullness of time, Bill Slim was determined to rectify.

Silberman, who had been polishing his glasses with a pocket handkerchief, suddenly tilted his head to one side and replaced them quickly, staring at the jungle.

"What's that?" he asked, with a touch of alarm that

made the other three grab their Thompson sub-machine guns and cock the weapons hurriedly.

Out of the undergrowth, with an immense amount of crashing and snapping, there emerged the front half of an elephant. Armstrong saw at once that it was wild, and not a domesticated working elephant; the latter had six inches of their tusks removed every year, and this beast's tusks were long and curved, ending in wickedly sharp points.

It ambled forward until all of it was visible, then stopped and surveyed them out of its piggy little eyes. Its ears, much smaller than those of an African elephant, flapped a couple of times, then flattened themselves along the sides of its skull.

"Oh, my God," Silberman breathed. "It's going to charge!"

Instinctively, they all raised their Tommy-guns and pointed them at the animal.

"Don't antagonise the goddam thing," one of the American pilots muttered.

The elephant took another couple of lumbering steps forward. It grunted.

Elephants don't grunt, Armstrong thought irrationally.

The beast eyed them for long seconds. Then, with what seemed very like a sorry shake of its head, it turned its broad rump towards them and, with a contemptuous flick of its scraggy tail, was gone.

Their laughter, as they climbed back into the jeep, was somewhat nervous.

Eleven

Magwe Aerodrome, 21 March 1942

The small group of men sat on empty upturned petrol cans outside the *basha*, the bamboo hut, that served as the operations room. Sticky Glew sat some distance away at a small table, on which his radio transceiver was perched. It derived its power from a generator that chugged away steadily, unseen around the far end of the hut.

"Any news, Sticky?" Armstrong asked for the tenth time. Glew looked up and shook his head.

"They must have bombed by now," Iggy Silberman commented. "We should have heard something."

They all shared his concern. On the previous day, a reconnaissance Hudson from Akyab had flown over Mingaladon, the former RAF and AVG base, and detected a build-up of Japanese bombers and fighters there. A force of nine Blenheims, ten Hurricanes and half a dozen P-40s – all that could be assembled – had been sent out from Magwe and Akyab to attack them as soon as possible the next morning.

Armstrong had wanted to take part in the mission, but he and his pilots had been absolutely forbidden to fly by the officer commanding Burwing, Group Captain Broughall.

"Be sensible, Armstrong," Broughall had told him. "You and your men have done more than your share. You are due to leave for India tomorrow. Air Vice-Marshal Stevenson would have my guts for garters if I authorised you to fly, and anything happened to you."

Armstrong was bitterly disappointed, but got the point. Still, it was a frustrating business, sitting things out while others did the fighting. After all, the AVG were still in the thick of it, and they'd done more than anybody.

Armstrong had relinquished command of the Magwe squadrons to a remarkable officer, Wing Commander Frank Carey. Like Armstrong, Carey had fought in the battles of France and Britain, during which he had destroyed eighteen enemy aircraft; unlike Armstrong, who came from Berwick-upon-Tweed, he was a Londoner, having been born in Brixton.

Carey had arrived in Burma as commanding officer of No. 135 Squadron, which Armstrong's squadron had relieved at Mingaladon. Sticky Glew had told Armstrong about a remarkable air combat he'd witnessed, a day or two before the replacement Hurricanes had flown in.

"The field had been bombed, and we had just crawled out of our slit trenches when two aircraft appeared. One was a Nakajima fighter, the other was Carey's Hurricane. Well, it was just like they were on a race track. Round and round the airdrome perimeter they went, kind of glued together, if you know what I mean, with the Hurricane chopping away at the Jap in short bursts. Bits fell off it and we could see bullets ripping into the area around the cockpit, but it was ages before it went down. The Jap pilot's body had twenty-seven bullets in it, and they reckon it was only the one that went through his head that finally brought him down."

"I can see them!" The cry came from Eamonn O'Day, who had been scanning the southern sky through binoculars. There was a pause, and his lips moved as he counted the incoming aircraft under his breath, then he exclaimed: "My stars, I think they're all there!"

They watched the aircraft come in to land; the fighters first, because they were low on fuel, and then the Blenheims. All were indeed back safely, although a few had bullet holes in them and one or two Blenheim crewmen had superficial bullet or shrapnel wounds.

A sweat-stained Roger Craig came up, his face creased in a grin.

"What a hell of a prang!" he said jubilantly. "Really brought the house down! We reckon we destroyed sixteen on the ground, and the fighter boys got quite a few, too."

The fighter pilots, in fact, had claimed eleven victories. The enemy had been taken completely by surprise, and most of their fighters had been destroyed as they were taking off or climbing to engage the bombers, when they were at a disadvantage.

Group Captain Broughall arrived in a jeep, raising a cloud of dust as he screeched to a stop in front of the *basha*. He clapped Craig on the back enthusiastically.

"Well done! Good show! Right, let's get you debriefed. There's no time to be lost. We'll take another crack at 'em this afternoon, while they're still on the hop."

Armstrong listened in as the bomber crews and fighter

pilots were debriefed, listening to their voices – the tones ranging from weary and monosyllabic to high-pitched and excited – as they told their stories to Silberman and an RAF Intelligence Officer.

"Stick of bombs went right across one group of bombers . . . blew 'em to kingdom come . . . Got one bastard as he was pulling his undercart up . . . went over on his back and dived straight in . . . shot one off Johnny's tail . . . broke up in mid-air . . . saw two collide . . . flew straight through the wreckage . . . thought I'd never make it . . . saw some Japs running like hell . . . gave 'em a good burst, nailed a couple . . ."

And so on. Armstrong smiled, recalling the Battle of Britain. How intelligence officers ever made sense out of the gabble of voices, how they managed to sort out the combat claims of individual pilots, he would never know. He did not envy them in their task.

"This is going to bring the Japs down on us like a ton of bricks," a familiar voice said into Armstrong's ear. "I hope we can take another good swipe at them first."

Armstrong turned and looked at Baird. "Whatever we do, it'll be no more than a pinprick," he said. "According to some intelligence estimates, the Japs have two hundred bombers in Siam and southern Burma. We've got what? Twenty at the most, split up between here and Akyab, with precious little hope of reinforcement. This show's just about over, I reckon."

"I agree." The speaker was the army major who had been with them at Mingaladon. "Without air support, we can't hope to hold on, even though our chaps on the ground are fighting like tigers. The Chinese, in particular. They've been fighting like the very devil at Toungoo for over a week now, holding on to the Sittang river crossing there. They've been asking us to relieve the pressure on them by staging some sort of demonstration on the Prome front, but how the hell we're going to do it, I just don't know. Trouble is, the Japanese commanders have never been to Staff College."

Armstrong raised a questioning eyebrow. "What do you mean?" he asked.

"I mean they don't fight by the book," the major explained. "Just when you think you're home and dry, you'll find that they've sneaked round behind you through the jungle and set up a road-block to cut you off. And since you are restricted to the roads because of your transport, you either have to leave it behind and go around the road-block via the jungle, or try to fight your way through."

"In which case, if there are a hundred at the road-block, you have to kill ninety-five before you've got a chance of breaking through."

The speaker was another army officer, a captain on the major's small liaison staff.

"Yes, and then those five would fight on until they ran out of ammunition, after which they'd commit suicide," the major added. "Ferocity and utter obedience, that's their code. It makes them a formidable army."

"It would make a European army invincible," Kalinski said quietly. Armstrong had almost forgotten about him. The Pole had been immersed in a book, and had taken

154

absolutely no notice of anything going on around him until now.

"And we were told the Japs were no good," O'Day interjected. "Remember all those tales about their aircraft – how they were made of cardboard, virtually, so that if you found yourself in trouble all you had to do was dive away so that their wings would fall off if they tried to follow you? And their pilots, all of whom had to wear glasses because they were so short-sighted?"

"Well, we know better now, don't we?" Kalinski said. "The question is, what are we going to do about it?"

Further speculation was cut abruptly short by the reappearance of Group Captain Broughall, whose gaze fell on Armstrong's small band. He waved Armstrong over.

"Just popped into my office to find a signal addressed to you, Armstrong. It seems you are urgently needed at Air HQ in Calcutta. You are to fly to Akyab, where a flying boat will pick you up. How many of your chaps are still here?"

"Only the four of us, sir. The others left a couple of days ago, along with the ground crews."

"Good. Well, Armstrong, you'd better get your kit together. You won't be coming back. I'll lay on a Lysander to take you to Akyab. Be ready for the off in half an hour."

Wondering what lay in store for them, Armstrong and the others collected their belongings, said a few hasty farewells, and were soon airborne in a Lysander flown by Mo Mukerjee himself. The Lysander was a large aircraft and had a roomy cockpit, but the Indian pilot had decided to create more space by leaving his gunner behind.

After crossing the Irrawaddy – where they noticed that the river was choked with refugee craft – and the comparatively flat and open strip of country that bordered it, Mukerjee climbed several thousand feet to rise above the razor-edged ridges of the Arakan Yomas, clad to their summits with dense jungle. They gave the impression of a thick, dull green carpet, rucked up into fold after fold.

Akyab airfield lay not far from the port itself. The commander of Akwing, Group Captain Singer, arranged for a car to take them to the harbour. An almost tearful Mukerjee bade them goodbye; he would take off on the return trip to Magwe once his aircraft had been refuelled.

At the harbour, a launch took them out to the waiting flying boat, an American-built Catalina belonging to the RAF's No. 205 Squadron. The squadron had once been based at Seletar, Singapore, and since the fall of that bastion it had led a nomadic existence, providing a courier service between India, Burma and the Dutch East Indies. Its pilot, who had been delivering mail and dispatches to Akwing HQ and who was anxious to be off, told Armstrong that the squadron expected to leave for Australia in the very near future.

Half an hour after take-off, the Catalina's wireless operator came forward and handed a slip of paper to the pilot, who glanced at it and then beckoned to Armstrong.

"Seems we got away just in time," he said. "Akyab and Magwe are both under attack."

Armstrong glanced at his watch. It was four hours since

they had left Magwe. The reprisal had come swiftly – or perhaps the raids had already been planned and on the point of taking place before the RAF attack on Mingaladon.

Flying Officer Mo Mukerjee saw the smoke rising from Magwe when he was still thirty miles away, and was filled with dread, for he knew it for what it was. Breathing a silent prayer for the safety of his comrades, he headed towards the dark beacon on the horizon. The miles crept by with agonising slowness. He called control, but there was no reply, for Sticky Glew was dead, a shapeless bundle under a blood-soaked blanket.

Mukerjee arrived overhead the airfield and looked down on a scene of utter devastation. The ground was littered with wrecked and burning aircraft; buildings lay in ruin. He managed to find a place to land, a crater-free area on the very edge of the strip, and in a few minutes he knew the worst.

Returning to his Lysander, he climbed back into the cockpit, and there, his head resting on his hands, Mo Mukerjee wept as he had never wept before. He wept for the destruction of his small command, which had survived numerous encounters with Japanese fighters in the air only to be wiped out on the ground, and for those of his officers and men who would never see another dawn.

And most of all he wept for his gunner, who, but for the pilot's last-minute decision, would now be among the living.

It was only the beginning. During the next twenty-four hours more than 230 Japanese aircraft attacked Magwe, destroying all but six Blenheims and eleven Hurricanes. These survivors were flown to Akyab, which so far had escaped comparatively lightly. The three remaining P-40s were flown to Lashio, on the Chinese border; the AVG ground personnel, among them Iggy Silberman, set off up the Irrawaddy, destination uncertain. They were accompanied by the few remaining RAF ground crews.

For Akyab it was to be only a temporary respite. A few days later the Japanese launched three devastating raids on the airfield; when they ended only four Hurricanes were left, and these were evacuated to India.

The Allied fighters in Burma had given a magnificent account of themselves: 233 enemy aircraft had fallen to them in air combat, with 76 probably destroyed and 116 damaged, together with 58 destroyed on the ground. The Allies had lost 38 aircraft in combat, 22 of them Hurricanes.

But it was over. The RAF and the American Volunteer Group had been driven from Burma, and the country's towns, together with the long columns of refugees and troops struggling towards India, were at the mercy of the Japanese Air Force.

Lieutenant-Colonel Ozawa had kept his promise.

Twelve

Calcutta, 23 March 1942

Armstrong's first impression of Air Vice-Marshal Stevenson was one of utter weariness. It was no wonder. Within weeks, if they continued to advance at their present rate, the Japanese would be at the frontier of Bengal, the very gateway to India. Stevenson had now been handed a new task. He was to organise the air defence of Calcutta, of the industrial centres of Bengal and Bihar, and of the vital oil installations at Digboi in Assam. Not only that: he was to establish a bomber force on bases in India for operations against the Japanese in Burma, and for attacks on enemy shipping in the Bay of Bengal.

Stevenson had set up a temporary headquarters in Government House, which was also used as a Mess by Army and RAF staff officers. He and Armstrong were conferring in one of the spacious sitting-rooms, ventilated by a slow-moving electric fan.

"You and your officers are overdue for a rest, Armstrong," Stevenson said, "but there simply isn't time. I'm sorry. I'm sending you south, to Ceylon, and you must be there by the beginning of April."

Armstrong showed his surprise. "Ceylon, sir?"

Stevenson nodded. "That's right. Let me explain the position. There are indications that a powerful Japanese fleet may even now be sailing for the Indian Ocean with the intention of attacking Ceylon. If the island's defences are overwhelmed, the enemy may well decide to land troops there as a springboard for the invasion of southern India – a very grave prospect indeed."

The Air Vice-Marshal paused and fiddled with a paper-knife that lay on a small table next to his armchair.

"At the moment," he continued, "Ceylon's only air defence consists of a few Royal Navy Fulmars – hardly the type of fighter capable of taking on the Zero on equal terms."

Armstrong mentally agreed. In service with the Royal Navy since 1940, the Fairey Fulmar was a monoplane fighter, like the Hurricane, and also like the Hurricane it carried an armament of eight machine guns. It had scored some success against Italian and German bombers attacking British convoys in the Mediterranean. However, the Fulmar had a top speed of only 270 miles per hour, which made it fifty miles per hour slower than the Hurricane – and seventy miles per hour slower than the Zero.

"The only ray of hope lies in the fact that thirty Hurricanes have just been landed at Karachi," Stevenson said. "They were originally destined for Singapore. However, they are in crates, and it will be some time before they are assembled and air tested. In the meantime, I must do something to strengthen Ceylon's air defences, and this is where you come in."

Armstrong stared at his superior impassively; he could make a shrewd guess as to what was coming next.

"You and your flight commanders, Armstrong, have a great deal of combat experience, far more than most pilots in this theatre. I am assigning six Hurricanes to you. They are presently at Dum Dum, so you'll have a long trip in store."

Dum Dum was an airstrip on the outskirts of Calcutta, near the township that had given its name to the infamous soft-nosed bullet that expanded on impact with the human body and caused horrendous wounds.

"I'll need more pilots, sir," Armstrong said. "Some of my squadron chaps are here in Calcutta; they were evacuated a few days ago, when we started running out of aircraft. Oh, and there's one other thing. There's a Flight Sergeant Cairns; he and his ground crews looked after us well in Burma. I'd like him along, too, but I don't know where to find him. He really is a first-rate type."

Stevenson nodded. "I'll have my personnel chaps winkle him out for you. He can have his pick of the airmen he needs. Oh, by the way, you'll be based at Ratlamana; that's the Ceylon Flying Club airfield."

The Air Vice-Marshal stood up, indicating that the interview was almost at an end.

"You'll form the nucleus of the Ceylon Air Defence Wing, Armstrong. With luck, the first eight Hurricanes of the reinforcement batch will be joining you by the end of the month. Also with luck, you'll have a few days to find out how their pilots measure up. They're all fresh out from the United Kingdom, and they haven't flown on operations yet."

Wonderful, Armstrong told himself. All he wants me to do is take on the cream of the Japanese Navy with a bunch of green kids. Not much to ask.

Kalinski and O'Day showed much the same reaction when he passed on the news to them half an hour later. Only Dickie Baird seemed pleased.

"Ceylon, eh?" he said with a broad smile. "Beautiful place! Nearest thing to paradise on earth, I'd say."

Armstrong looked sideways at him.

"And when were you there, Dickie?" he asked mildly.

"Oh, 1937. Came out on a supply ship. Part of my seamanship training. I was only a midshipman then."

"And how long were you here, Dickie?" Armstrong wanted to know.

"Oh, just a week," Baird replied, without thinking. His mind was busy with the sudden realisation that 1937 was only five years ago; in that time he had jumped in rank from midshipman to lieutenant-commander, a step that would have taken three times as long in peacetime.

"A week! You must have really got to know Ceylon in that time, Dickie!"

They laughed. Baird smiled wryly, conscious that he had indulged in a bit of low-key 'line-shooting' and that fun was being poked at him as a consequence.

"It's been a while," he said.

"Since what?"

"Since we had a bit of a laugh. Go on, make the most of it. There's not much to laugh at, here in Calcutta."

He was right in that. They had been there only twenty-four hours, and yet they had already come to realise that Calcutta was a city of contrast. At one extreme was blatant wealth, at the other squalid misery that went far beyond mere poverty. There were cinemas, restaurants and clubs as opulent as any to be found in Europe; there were disease-ridden brothels where families sold a daughter or a sister into slavery to earn a few extra rupees.

And there was civil unrest, its flames fanned by a skinny little man called Gandhi, who advocated civil disobedience and passive resistance to the British administration throughout India. There was the Congress Party, too, whose agents whipped up rabid anti-British feeling, urged all Indians to refrain from the war effort, and tried to tempt Indian troops to desert.

The leaders of the Congress Party, many of whom had a naïve belief that if the Japanese Army overran India it would install them as a puppet government and withdraw, were arrested and imprisoned, as was Gandhi. The result was that the anti-British campaign was taken over by militants, and violence flared up throughout Bengal.

It had not yet affected Calcutta to any great extent, but there were signs that it would. Widespread disturbances broke out in several towns; trams were burned (which, Armstrong was told, was the usual signal that a full-scale riot was about to begin) and there were student demonstrations.

All in all, Armstrong and the others had no wish to sample the delights of Calcutta. It was a relief when, after spending the night at Government House, transport arrived to take them to Dum Dum early the next morning. By this time they had been joined by the two extra pilots assigned to them by AHQ: one was the New Zealander, Flying Officer Robinson; the other, to Armstrong's surprise, was Peter Crabtree, the Hurricane pilot who had turned up at Mingaladon after escaping from Singapore. His injured arm was now healed and he was fully recovered from his experience.

Arrangements had been made for the ground crews – Cairns and his men having been located after some difficulty – to fly to Ceylon in a transport aircraft, together with some other passengers who were going in that direction.

The Hurricanes took off from Dum Dum – a dreadful place, nothing more than a stretch of beaten ground with a few huts on it into the rose-pearl light of an Indian dawn. A lone Blenheim was circling over Calcutta; it turned south as they came up and they formated on it, three Hurricanes taking station in loose formation off each wingtip. The Blenheim was going to Ceylon too, and its crew would look after the navigation.

Ahead of them lay a flight of 1,400 miles, with refuelling stops *en route*; 1,400 miles following the western coastline of the Bay of Bengal, during which they would see many changes of scenery, from the many mouths of the sacred Ganges in the north to the slopes of the Nilgiris in the south-east, rising to 8,000 feet and abundant in teak, ebony, satinwood and sandalwood. And on to Ceylon itself, with its tumbling waterfalls, its forests, jungle and scrub, lying like a coral-fringed jewel at the foot of the subcontinent.

A few hours behind the Blenheim and Hurricanes, Flight Sergeant Cairns was also admiring the scenery from his seat in the passenger cabin of a Douglas DC-2 transport. It belonged to No. 31 Squadron of the Royal Air Force, based at Lahore. A few weeks earlier it had been one of several used by KLM, the Royal Netherlands Airline, to carry passengers and freight between Amsterdam and Batavia. Now the Japanese held Batavia, and the DC-2s that had escaped to India were operated by the RAF.

The DC-2 was fast and comfortable, a far cry indeed from the old, lumbering Vickers Valentia biplanes which had previously equipped the squadron. Its twin Wright Cyclone engines droned sweetly, producing a soporific effect that Cairns found hard to resist.

In fact, if it were not for the interesting conversation of the passenger who sat next to him, he would almost certainly have been asleep. She was in charge of four nurses who were travelling to take up posts at a military hospital in Ceylon's capital, Colombo.

It was the most amazing coincidence, the fatherly Cairns thought, that this attractive young nursing sister should know Wing Commander Armstrong.

Thirteen

At Sea, South Of Java, 1 April 1942

Vice-Admiral Chuichi Nagumo, commanding the Japanese First Carrier Fleet, stood with his feet braced apart on the bridge of his flagship, the aircraft carrier *Akagi*, and scanned the horizon though his cherished pair of Zeiss binoculars. Through their splendid optics the warships of his fleet leaped into crisp focus.

This was the fleet which, just under four months earlier, had dealt the killing blow against the American Pacific Fleet at Pearl Harbor. It was a pity, Nagumo thought, that the American aircraft carriers, which had been at sea at the time, had escaped; sooner or later he would have to fight them and destroy them. They, and their aircraft, were the Americans' only means of striking at Japan's newly conquered possessions in the Pacific and Indian Oceans.

What a magnificent sight the warships made, and what honourable names they bore! Here, vibrating under his feet, was his own *Akagi*, the 'Red Castle'; and over there Rear-Admiral Yamaguchi's *Hiryu*, the 'Flying Dragon', leading the Second Carrier Squadron. In the distance, he could make out three more flat-tops: the *Soryu*, 'Blue

Dragon'; *Zuikaku*, 'Lucky Crane'; and finally the *Shokaku*, the 'Happy Crane'.

Their colourful names belied the destruction this formidable task force was capable of dealing out. Between them, the five ships carried nearly 400 bombers and fighters. And other immensely powerful warships were included in the task force, too.

Over on the southern flank were the four mighty warships of Rear-Admiral Mikawa's Third Battleship Squadron, steaming in line astern. First came the 32,000-ton *Kongo*; then her three sister ships, the *Haruna*, *Hiyei* and *Kirishima*, all named after sacred mountains in Japan. They had originally been built as battlecruisers just before the Great War, but after substantial rebuilding they had been re-classified as battleships.

Scouting ahead of the fleet, out of sight over the horizon, were the cruisers *Tone*, *Chikuma* and *Abukuma*, and guarding the task force's flanks, like scurrying dogs, were nine destroyers. As added protection, six submarines were now sailing from Penang, in Malaya, to take up covering positions to the west of India.

Nagumo was supremely confident that the Imperial Japanese Navy, under the direction of its able commander, Admiral Isoroku Yamamoto, would triumph over the Allies wherever and whenever it encountered them. But it was a pity that the Allies, instead of taking the sensible course of action and seeking a negotiated peace after the sweeping Japanese victories of the past few months, were fighting back.

Nagumo had always doubted that the British and

Americans would give in. Especially the British, who had been fighting against hopeless odds, alone, for nearly two years before the Germans attacked Russia. The Americans had already struck back, with raids on Japanese bases in the Marshall and Gilbert Islands by aircraft from their troublesome carriers, the *Enterprise*, *Yorktown* and *Lexington*, formed into task forces under two tough and capable commanders, Vice-Admiral William Halsey and Rear-Admiral Frank Fletcher; and Rabaul had been attacked by aircraft based in Australia.

Yamamoto had ordered Nagumo to teach the Australians a lesson, and in mid-February his carriers had launched seventy-one dive-bombers and eighty-one torpedo bombers, escorted by thirty-six Zeros, in a devastating attack on the North Australian harbour of Port Darwin. Nagumo had been well satisfied with the result: nine large merchant ships and one Australian destroyer had been sunk, along with four smaller craft. The air defences had been pitifully weak.

He did not expect Ceylon's air defences to be much better.

Nagumo's chief signals officer appeared suddenly at his elbow and saluted, waiting for the admiral to acknowledge him before handing him a slip of paper. Nagumo looked at it and nodded with satisfaction.

The decoded signal told him that Imperial Navy's Malaya Force, under his friend Vice-Admiral Ozawa, had put to sea from Mergui in Burma with the aircraft carrier *Ryujo*, five heavy cruisers, a light cruiser and four destroyers, its task to attack shipping in the Bay of Bengal.

168

Good, Nagumo thought. That should keep Admiral Somerville busy. The Japanese admiral had made it his business to study the enemy naval commanders, and he knew all there was to know about Admiral Sir James Somerville. He also knew, through the daily intelligence summary – which was flashed to all commanders from Tokyo, and which was always extremely accurate and up to date – that Admiral Somerville had taken command of the British Eastern Fleet a few days ago.

On an impulse, he turned to one of the junior officers who happened to be on watch and rapped out an order. The man hurried off, and a minute later returned with a folder. Nagumo opened it and studied its contents. They consisted of two sheets of paper, on which was typed the Eastern Fleet's order of battle as it appeared two days earlier. The Japanese spy network was functioning well.

Somerville had, under his command, two large aircraft carriers and a small one. The large vessels were the *Indomitable* and *Formidable*; the small one was the *Hermes*.

Nagumo had made a careful study of these vessels, which were described at great length in that excellent and informative English publication, *Jane's Fighting Ships*. He knew that they could carry up to seventy-two aircraft, but doubted whether they had the full complement on board. Even if they did, his own air power outnumbered the enemy's by nearly three to one, and his aircraft were far more modern. He knew also, according to the intelligence summary, that the *Hermes*'s air group was disembarked and ashore at Katakarunda, in Ceylon.

Had he but known the full facts, Nagumo might have dismissed Somerville's air power out of hand. Between them, the British carriers had no more than fifty-seven strike aircraft and forty fighters, all of them obsolete by Japanese standards.

Nagumo's main concern was the five battleships which Somerville had at his disposal: the *Warspite*, *Ramillies*, *Resolution*, *Revenge* and *Royal Sovereign*. They were all elderly, having been built during the last war, but like his own battleships they had been modernised. If, by some unfortunate chance, they found themselves in a position to intercept his fleet while his air cover was absent, they might inflict terrible damage on it. And, as well as the big ships, the British Eastern Fleet had seven cruisers, sixteen destroyers and a few submarines.

Nagumo's intention was to destroy the Eastern Fleet in its base at Trincomalee, to inflict a crushing defeat on the British, as he had done on the Americans at Pearl Harbor.

Admiral Somerville's intention was that no such thing must be allowed to happen. And Somerville had a powerful weapon in his arsenal. The Americans had cracked the Japanese Navy's basic code, and since Pearl Harbor they had been sharing its secrets with the British.

The signals that had flashed between Tokyo and the First Carrier Fleet had been intercepted by Allied wireless monitoring stations, and their secrets decoded. Somerville did not yet know the exact location of Nagumo's fleet. But he had known for three days now that it was coming, and that Ceylon was its target. And it was for that reason that he had dispersed his main fleet, sending the capital ships and aircraft carriers to a secret base at Addu Atoll in the Maldive Islands, south-west of Ceylon. Furthermore, he had divided his warships into two battle squadrons: Force A, the fast group, comprising the battleship *Warspite*, the two fleet carriers and the more modern cruisers and destroyers, and Force B, made up of the older and slower vessels.

It was up to the RAF's long-range Catalina reconnaissance aircraft now. Only they could pinpoint the enemy fleet with precision and pass on the vital information to Somerville, so that he could marshal his forces and bring the enemy to battle.

If he failed, nothing lay between the enemy bombers and the destruction of Colombo but a handful of RAF and Fleet Air Arm fighters, outnumbered by five to one.

In Ceylon, Armstrong could only guess at the kind of odds that might be stacked against him and his fellow pilots. He had spent the last week devising tactics to cope with the strong possibility that his small fighter force would be heavily outnumbered at all times. He had decided to divide his fighter force; assuming that it would be able to get off the ground unharmed and have plenty of warning, the intention was that half the available Hurricanes would join the Navy's Fulmars in engaging the Japanese bombers, while the remaining Hurricanes kept the fighters busy.

The tactics had worked well in the Battle of Britain, when Spitfires had taken on the German fighter escort while the Hurricanes had attacked the bombers. But there were no Spitfires in Ceylon.

The one encouraging fact was that his Hurricane force had been increasing daily, as the fighters were assembled at Karachi, air-tested and sent on their way to swell the ranks in Ceylon. In fact, the little airstrip at Ratlamana had become too overcrowded for safety, so the new arrivals were being diverted to Colombo racecourse, on the other side of town.

Armstrong wished that he could have more time with Philippa, but with his fighters on full alert he did not dare spend too much time away from base, and in any case she was hard at work setting up more emergency treatment facilities at the hospital in town. With the experience of Burma to draw on, she knew full well what she and her staff might have to cope with, when the Japanese attack came.

He wasn't sure of his feelings for Philippa. She wasn't quiet – in fact, she was amazingly knowledgeable about lots of things, and a good conversationalist – but there was a certain reserve about her that was almost a barrier, and he had no idea how to break through.

She was certainly nothing like Phyllis, the blonde, big-busted landlady of the Pyewype Inn on the outskirts of Cambridge. She would have had him well tucked in by now. Armstrong suddenly realised with a small shock that it was over a year since he'd seen Phyllis, just before his departure for the Middle East. He had heard from her a couple of times, by way of letters written in large, rounded script that had made him shake his head and chuckle; but it was not literary ability that had attracted him to her in the first place, and they both knew it. She knew she would never be invited; he knew that she had a circle of friends he would never meet, either. They enjoyed one another when circumstance and war permitted, and that was that.

He would always remember Phyllis with fondness and gratitude. Philippa was something else.

Armstrong was glad that Flight Sergeant Cairns had told him straight away that Philippa was in Colombo, and where, and he hadn't missed the twinkle in the NCO's eye. He had rung her at once, and learned that she had been about to call him, and so they had arranged to meet. Together, they had strolled through the Pettah, the outer suburb of Colombo south of the harbour that was the hub of the city's traditional markets. To Armstrong, the narrow streets, with their small shops jumbled almost on top of one another, had seemed claustrophobic, but his companion found them fascinating.

Philippa Windrush knew a great deal about Colombo in particular, and Ceylon in general. He was not in the least surprised when Philippa told him that she had spent the first fifteen years of her life there. Nothing surprised him any more.

"My father was a Methodist minister," she told him. "He used to work terribly hard, even though his health wasn't very good. We actually lived in Kandy, up in the hills. Why father chose to live there, I never found out, because it's the biggest Buddhist stronghold in Ceylon. Perhaps he really wanted to achieve something by making converts there. It's where they keep the Tooth Relic," she added with a little smile.

"The what?"

173

"The Tooth Relic. It's supposed to be one of the Buddha's teeth, but I find that a little hard to believe, because it's a good three inches long and it looks like discoloured ivory."

"Can anyone see it?" Armstrong wanted to know.

Philippa shook her head. "No, the monks only bring it out once in a while, and then only to be seen by royal visitors and the faithful. It's kept in the Temple of the Tooth; that's next to the esplanade, overlooking Kandy Lake."

She paused as they came to a crossroads. The crowd was thinning out now, for which Armstrong was grateful.

"Let's go down here," Philippa said. "That road leads to the harbour. This one comes out Marine Drive, just by the lighthouse."

"Please go on about the Tooth," Armstrong prompted.

"Oh, yes. Well, when it's known that the Tooth is about to be exhibited, a vast crowd of worshippers of all ages crams the temple courtyard. They bring offerings with them – young coconut leaves, scent, flowers, fruit, all those sorts of things. They wait for many hours, sometimes. Then the main temple door is opened and they all surge up a dark, narrow stairway that leads to a pair of silver and ivory doors. When these are opened, a flood of hot, scented air pours out."

She paused to wave and smile at a Sinhalese passer-by who called out a greeting to her, explaining to Armstrong that the man was a hospital porter, then resumed her story.

"The Tooth Relic is enclosed in five golden caskets,

or Karanduas, some of which are encrusted with rubies, emeralds or diamonds, and each of these is removed slowly and solemnly by the monks. The crowd can't come any closer, because the room is sealed off by gilded bars, and by this time they are all down on their knees, anyway. When the last Karandua comes off there's the Tooth, lying on a bed of red silk. The head priest lifts it by means of a golden thread and places it in a golden vessel shaped like a lotus, lifts it high with a sharp cry, and that's the signal for the other priests to beat their drums and blow on their conches and pipes. Then it goes back into the caskets and there's a ceremonial parade around the temple, led by elephants dressed up in their best."

Not for the first time, Armstrong shook his head in wonder at the diverse religious customs and beliefs of the human race. Thinking back to the *nats*, the mythical fairies of Burma, he hoped that the Tooth had the power to ward off evil spirits. The evil spirits were on their way, and they were coming in aircraft carriers.

The thought had jerked him back to reality, as he and Philippa stood on the broad path between the sea and the lawns that bordered Beira Lake and looked out over the Indian Ocean. The enemy was out there somewhere; but exactly where, no one knew as yet. They had stood there for a long while, savouring the sea breeze, before strolling across the lawns where children played.

In Burma, children were dying of cholera, their bodies stacked in heaps to be doused in petrol and burned.

Across the lawn a woman in a colourful sari ran,

laughing, trailing a kite, with two children clamouring behind her.

In Burma, beside the long road that led north, the rags of what had once been a colourful sari shrouded the bones of what had once been a woman, picked clean by ants and other creatures.

At the door of the hospital they said goodbye, both knowing that it might be for ever. Philippa's hand rested briefly in Armstrong's; it was the only contact there had been between them. But their eyes said everything, and it was enough.

Both of them knew, now. If there was to be a tomorrow, it would be theirs.

Fourteen

The Indian Ocean, 4 April 1942

L ieutenant Toru Saito stood stiffly to attention on the bridge of the *Akagi* and gave the Fleet Commander a crisp salute. Admiral Nagumo acknowledged it and nodded in greeting.

"Welcome aboard, Saito. I expect you are glad to be back at sea."

"Yes, sir. I await the admiral's orders."

Saito was indeed glad to feel a ship under him again, and to feel a clean sea breeze on his face after the heat and filth of Burma. It had come as a surprise when his squadron had been ordered to join *Akagi*; if anything, he had expected to return to the *Ryujo*. But combat losses, together with some deck-landing accidents, had reduced the carrier's fighter complement, and Nagumo needed reinforcements for the forthcoming operation. Saito did not mind; he had plenty of friends on *Akagi*. The Japanese Naval Air Arm was a tightly knit brotherhood.

Mechanics were fussing over his twelve Zeros, ranging them alongside other aircraft at the side of the flight deck. His pilots had already disappeared into the bowels of the ship, intent on freshening up and finding something to eat.

It had been a long flight from Burma down the Malay peninsula to Sumatra, topping up with fuel as they went – British fuel, found on captured airfields – and the last leg, the long haul south over the ocean, had taxed them to the limit of their skill. But they were Navy pilots, Saito thought proudly, and they had found the task force exactly where it was supposed to be.

Admiral Nagumo dismissed Saito, who thankfully allowed himself to be led to the quarters that had been made ready for him. More weary than hungry, he stripped, showered and was fast asleep in ten minutes, oblivious to the activity that suddenly brought the ship alive around him.

For not only he and his pilots had found Nagumo's task force. Twenty miles away, an alert lookout in a Catalina flying boat, one of half a dozen that had been patrolling constantly for the past four days over a great arc of sea to the south of Ceylon, spotted a smudge of smoke on the horizon. Slipping closer, making use of what scant cloud cover was available, the pilot and his seven-man crew were soon left in no doubt about what they were seeing.

Methodically, the wireless operator began tapping out the signal that would bring the Ceylon defences to their highest state of alert.

Already, the pilot could see the Zeros, glittering in the sun as they swept down upon him. He knew that in a matter of minutes, he and his men would meet a violent death. Behind him, the wireless operator remained at his post, sending out the stream of dots and dashes that would be his epitaph. It was 1500 hours.

In Colombo, the Roman Catholic cathedral of Santa Lucia was packed to capacity, for this was Easter Saturday. Some of the worshippers were military and naval personnel; among them were Lieutenant-Commander Dickie Baird and Flight Lieutenant Stanislaw Kalinski.

At his headquarters in Trincomalee, Admiral Sir Geoffrey Layton, the Commander-in-Chief, Ceylon, was asked by one of his staff if all personnel should be recalled immediately. The admiral shook his head.

"No. Let them finish their divine service."

He thought of the flying-boat crew, whose message had just come in. There had been no second signal. Poor devils.

At sea, the sighting report reached Admiral Sir James Somerville, whose warships had been concentrated to the south of Ceylon in anticipation of the Japanese attack. Two days ago, with no sign of anything developing, he had decided to return to allow normal shipping movements to resume and to return to Addu Atoll to refuel. He had almost arrived when he received the Catalina's one and only signal. The Japanese task force was 360 miles from Ceylon, almost within striking distance.

Somerville was going to need every available warship. Earlier, he had detached the heavy cruisers *Dorsetshire* and *Cornwall* and sent them to Trincomalee, along with the light carrier *Hermes*. He now instructed them to rejoin the fleet, but Admiral Layton had anticipated his need. The harbours at Colombo and Trincomalee were already being cleared of shipping, and the three warships were making ready to sail.

Armstrong's available fighter force now numbered fifty aircraft, thirty-six of them Hurricanes and the rest Fulmars. He decided to reserve the older and slower aircraft, the Fulmars and the Mk I Hurricanes, for the defence of Colombo; with the remainder, he would try to engage the enemy as far out to sea as possible, even to the limit of the Hurricane Mk II's combat radius.

The pilots all knew what that meant. In the event of a prolonged air battle, they might not have enough fuel left to get back to base.

All the more modern fighters were now assembled at Ratlamana, under Armstrong's direct control. Dickie Baird, who had chosen to fly a Fairey Fulmar, was in command at Colombo Racecourse.

At least, Armstrong thought, they ought to have plenty of warning of the enemy's approach, because there was a radar station on the southern tip of Ceylon, and it was functioning and linked to HQ in Colombo.

The question was not *if* the enemy would come, but when, and it was uppermost in Admiral Somerville's mind as his warships hurriedly replenished at Addu Atoll, 400 miles to the south-west of Ceylon. It was the most southerly of the Maldive Group, forty miles south of the Equator, and consisted of a circlet of small islands enclosing a lagoon that measured ten miles from east to west and six and a half miles from north to south. The islands were flat and low-lying, being rarely more than five feet above sea-level; the lagoon itself formed a magnificent natural harbour, with a depth of between twenty and forty fathoms.

It was part of the domain of His Majesty Sultan Hasan Noor-ud-Din, 'Lord of the Thousand Isles', although in fact he was lord over 200 inhabited ones and an unknown number, variously estimated from 2,000 to 12,000, that were uninhabited.

The few thousand people who lived on the islands encircling the lagoon eked out a precarious existence by fishing, harvesting coconuts and growing vegetables. As the shadows began to lengthen on this fourth day of April, Many of them looked on in awe at the procession of warships, led by the mighty battleship *Warspite* and the carriers *Indomitable* and *Formidable*, that nosed their way out into the Indian Ocean between the islands of Gan and Wilingili.

That night it rained. For two hours a downpour of incredible intensity lashed south-west Ceylon, drenching Armstrong's precious airstrips and threatening to make them inoperable. Neither he nor his pilots slept that night, discounting a fitful doze in the armchairs of the Ceylon Flying Club; it would have been difficult to do so anyway, because of the drumming of rain on the roof. It added to the tension, which was building unbearably. Armstrong had seen it all before; many of the other pilots had not. It would disappear as soon as they got airborne, but no amount of reassurance would convince them of that.

Two hundred and seventy-five miles south-east of Ceylon, the sky was clear. The *Akagi* had increased to maximum speed and a thirty-knot wind blasted down her flight deck. From the cockpit of his Zero, Toru Saito watched the Aichi D3A dive bombers, each bearing a

500-pound bomb slung under its fuselage, lumber into the air one by one. More bombers were taking off from the other carriers. In all, there were ninety of them.

The last Aichi rose from the flight deck, silhouetted against a rosy pre-dawn twilight. Then it was Saito's turn. Obeying the signals of the deck officer, he opened the throttle a little and the Zero moved slowly forward, the two sailors clinging to its wingtips helping him to turn the fighter and line it up properly.

He ran up the engine to full power, holding the stick back in the pit of his stomach. The deck officer's arm came down in a chopping motion and Saito released the brakes, at the same time releasing the backward pressure on the stick. The fighter's tail came up almost immediately and the Zero gathered speed along the flight deck, seeming to rise of its own volition. He raised the undercarriage and flaps, adjusted the propeller setting and climbed in the wake of the bombers.

Behind him, eleven other Zeros of his squadron followed in their turn. He felt proud that the Air Group Commander had given the squadron the honour of leading the escort, which was to comprise thirty-six Zeros.

Ahead of him, the bombers were settling into their V-shaped formation as they climbed. He looked over to the right, then hurriedly pulled his tinted goggles over his eyes as a bright orange sun burst into view above the horizon. Its glow matched the *hinomarus* on the wings of his fighter. Somehow, it seemed a good omen.

Climbing to 10,000 feet, the 126 aircraft set course for Ceylon.

0730 hours. At Dundra Head, on the southernmost tip of Ceylon, a small cluster of tents stood beside a large square steel trailer with narrow slatted windows. On the roof of the trailer was a large parabolic aerial shaped like an electric bowl fire, the antenna of an SCR 260B radar set. There was a muted hum from the generator that fed power to it.

Inside the trailer, one of the two RAF NCOs on duty gave a loud yawn. His companion looked at him and grinned.

"Not to worry, Joe. Another half-hour and we're off watch. Then we can crawl into our nice, damp blankets and get a spot of shut-eye."

Joe grimaced, and made no reply. He was fed up with being stuck out here, day after day, with nothing but seabirds and three other blokes for company. The two on the other watch would be up and about shortly. He glanced at the shimmering oscilloscope in front of him; it never showed anything other than interference and an occasional blip that was one of the search Catalinas, heading for or returning from its patrol area.

There was one now, at the extreme right-hand edge of the screen, right at the top, bearing zero-one-zero degrees. It was quite clear for a moment, then it faded. Joe logged it automatically, then looked at the previous entry he had made and frowned.

There was no Catalina operating in that sector.

The blip returned, perfectly sharp this time, transparent and green. Joe prodded his companion.

"Take a look at this, will you? What d'you reckon?"

"Lord, it's big! I'd say it was heading towards us, too."

"Plot it, quick!"

The airman quickly placed a sheet of transparent squared paper over the map on his plotting board, stuck a pin through the middle over their own location, and rapidly plotted the movement of the blip as Joe reeled off the information. With his other hand he manipulated a circular slide rule, calculating the speed of the incoming aircraft. They were doing about 220 miles an hour, and they were about 70 miles away. At that rate, they would be here in twenty minutes.

Joe could not afford to wait any longer. He reached for the telephone that linked him with the duty officer at HQ in Colombo. Within two minutes, the telephone bell was shrilling in the Ceylon Flying Club. Armstrong grabbed it, listened for a second, then gave an ear-splitting yell.

"Scramble! One hundred plus, sixty miles, angels ten!"

It took less than ten seconds to empty the building.

In the streets of Colombo, worshippers heading for early Mass on this Easter Sunday morning paused and looked up, startled, as the fighters roared overhead, climbing furiously into the southern sky. Some came from the direction of the flying club, others from the racecourse.

The people had never seen so many fighters in the air at one time before. And they noticed something else, too; the crews of the anti-aircraft guns sited at various points in the city were bustling around inside their sandbagged emplacements, making sure their ammunition was stacked handily. All were wearing their steel helmets.

The worshippers began walking again, more quickly now, heading for the cathedral. A minute later, the air raid warning sounded. The walk turned into a run. It was important to reach the cathedral before the bombers came. They would be safe there. No bombs would strike the house of God.

Few of them had heard of Coventry.

Armstrong had twenty fighters behind him; the rest were patrolling off the coast at 18,000 feet. Armstrong took his formation up to 20,000, searching ahead. Far beneath his fighter's wings the ocean was a deep green, shot here and there with flecks of white.

"Bandits one o'clock, low." That was Eamonn O'Day, keen-eyed as ever. And there they were, slightly off to the right, looking for all the world like several straggling gaggles of geese.

"Okay, but watch it. The escort will be around somewhere," Armstrong cautioned. The sun made it hard to see, and the Japs had it more or less at their backs.

"Jumbo Leader, this is Jumbo Yellow Two." That was Peter Crabtree. "I see them, twelve o'clock high, twenty plus."

"Roger. Jumbo Yellow Section, upstairs fast." The six Hurricanes of Yellow Section lifted away, clawing for altitude in order to engage the escort. The enemy fighters were a good 4,000 feet higher up.

Yellow Section was led by Kalinski, whose voice now came over the R/T. He told his pilots to pass under the Japanese fighters, still climbing, and manoeuvre into position up-sun of them, gaining the altitude advantage

185

before attacking. To attack on the climb would be suicidal, for the nimble Zeros would have all the advantages.

The two opposing formations were closing fast now. Twelve Hurricanes were left to take on nearly a hundred bombers. Oh, well, Armstrong told himself, we've faced these kind of odds before.

He ordered his pilots into the attack. They went down in pairs, very fast, so that the combined closing speed of the fighters and bombers was close on 600 miles per hour. At that velocity, there was no margin for error – only a split second to line up one's fighter, loose off a one-second burst, then dive hard beneath the other aircraft before climbing like a rocket for a second attempt, this time from astern.

In that split second, Armstrong automatically registered fine details of the bomber he was engaging, his mind noting that it had a single radial engine and a fixed undercarriage. It carried twin white bands around its rear fuselage, just behind the 'meatball', and it was a type unknown to him. He had no idea that this was one of the types that had inflicted such appalling damage at Pearl Harbor.

One day, the Allies would give the Aichi D3A the code-name 'Val'.

At the top of his climb, Armstrong made an Immelmann turn – a manoeuvre developed by and named after the famous German flying ace of the Great War – and dived hard to bring himself back into the fight, looking for another target. He could not see what had become of the first, but at least two bombers were heading vertically for the ocean, streaming flame and smoke.

Several thousand feet higher up, Lieutenant Toru Saito saw the glare and the smoke trails and realised for the first time that the bombers were under attack. He had not seen the British fighters coming in, and neither, apparently, had anyone else. Enraged, he screamed into his microphone, ordering his squadron to dive to the bombers' assistance. The twelve Zeros plummeted down, to be followed by the two other squadrons that were flying some distance behind.

All Saito could think of, as he set his sights on a Hurricane, was how he might redeem his loss of face.

The Hurricane Saito had spotted was Armstrong's. The RAF pilot had dived back into the fray and was attacking another Aichi from a range of only fifty yards, having knocked out its rear gunner. It was already burning.

The frenzy of rage and hatred that swept through Saito lasted only a fraction of a second before it was replaced by an icy calm. He opened the throttle and put his Zero into a long, sweeping dive, intent on the destruction of the other aircraft.

Suddenly, another Hurricane swept into view. It was flown by Armstrong's number two, a young New Zealander called McIver, who had experienced some difficulty in following his leader's manoeuvre and who was only now dropping into position astern, from where he could protect Armstrong's tail.

He didn't see the menace screaming down on him, and probably never knew what hit him.

Saito gave a slight push on the left rudder pedal to bring the Zero into line with McIver's Hurricane, waited until the British fighter filled his sights, and let fly with cannon and machine guns. His twenty-millimetre shells found their mark. Several of them tore through the cockpit and pilot, went on to penetrate the instrument panel and the firewall on the other side, and exploded in the fuselage fuel tank, which lay between the firewall and the engine.

Transformed into a ball of fire, the Hurricane curved away towards the sea, trailing a dense streamer of smoke that was mingled with a white trail of glycol from the ruptured engine coolant tank.

Not far away, another ball of flame fell vertically. Armstrong did not pause to watch his victim's doom; instead, he steep turned away, and the manoeuvre probably saved his life.

Saito's burst of shells and bullets tore through the Hurricane's slipstream, missing the aircraft by a few feet. The Japanese pilot, furious with himself, hauled back the stick, almost blacking out as the Zero came out of its dive and bounded skywards.

Saito pulled the fighter up into the first stage of a loop, bending his head backwards to keep the Hurricane in sight, and half-rolled off the top. As he did so, the shadow of his aircraft flickered across Armstrong's cockpit.

Startled, Armstrong looked up and saw the Zero a few hundred feet above, its wings waggling as its pilot prepared to dive to the attack. The enemy held every conceivable advantage except one. The heavier Hurricane could out-dive him. Armstrong did not hesitate. Pushing the stick forward, he sent his aircraft plummeting towards the Indian Ocean.

The airspeed rose rapidly, as rapidly as the altimeter needle was unwinding. A glance behind told Armstrong that the Zero was still following, but that he was outrunning it. At 3,000 feet, ever so gently, he began to ease the stick back. The air battle had brought them close to Ceylon, and the island was dead ahead. Up above, the bombers that had escaped the fighter attacks – and there were still a great many of them – were heading relentlessly towards Colombo.

One thousand feet. The Zero was still behind, but Armstrong knew that he had enough room for the manoeuvre he intended to perform.

All right, you bastard, he thought. Now let's see about it.

In the Zero's cockpit, Toru Saito suddenly tensed as the aircraft in front of him appeared to lose speed. His lips parted in a grimace of triumph. I have you now, Englishman, he told himself.

At that precise moment the Englishman did something quite unexpected. He pulled his fighter up into a barrel roll, losing even more speed. It was a manoeuvre Armstrong had practised time and again, and used to good effect in combat. It all depended on split-second timing, and on the pursuer having excessive speed.

Saito's Zero shot straight through the middle of Armstrong's roll. He looked back in sudden panic, just in time to see the Hurricane curving round on his tail as Armstrong completed the manoeuvre, increasing speed again. The two aircraft were practically down to sea level and Armstrong's bullets whipped up flurries of spray around the Zero as he opened fire. With very little ammunition left, he knew that he had to get it right first time.

Desperately, Saito flung the Zero into a tight turn, and flew straight into Armstrong's second burst of fire. The stick in his hand went slack as bullets severed the control cables. Saito had just enough time to commend his spirit to his ancestors before the Zero flew into the sea at 200 miles per hour.

Armstrong glanced at his fuel gauges; he barely had enough left to get back to the airfield. He could see smoke rising from the direction of Colombo. In a strange, detached way, he didn't care. His head was swimming, and he found himself shaking and sweating. Reaction, he supposed, but he'd never felt quite like it before, and the fact worried him.

By the time he came within sight of Ratlamana, he was shivering with cold. Taking no notice of frantic calls over the R/T, warning him not to land because of the presence of enemy aircraft – he had no choice anyway, because of his fuel state – he throttled back, slid back the cockpit canopy, changed the propeller pitch and almost forgot to lower the undercarriage.

The mainwheels hit the ground and the Hurricane bounced twice before settling down. Armstrong closed the throttle and sat slumped in his seat, unable to move. Some airmen came running up; one of them jumped up on the wing and peered at the pilot.

"Are you wounded, sir?" he asked urgently.

Armstrong looked up at him, barely able to focus his eyes.

"Don't think so," he said weakly. "Help me to get out, will you?"

Another airman joined the first. They unfastened Armstrong's seat and parachute harnesses and lifted him bodily from the cockpit. Waving them aside, he slid off the trailing edge of the wing and stood upright.

Earth and sky gyrated around one another for a sickening second, then the world went black.

Fifteen

"What's wrong with me?" Armstrong asked, struggling to sit up. He clearly remembered collapsing on the airfield, and for a confused moment thought he was still there. Then he realised that he was in a hospital bed.

"You've got a particularly nasty brand of malaria, old chap," a familiar voice. "That, combined with exhaustion, has pretty well done you in. How are you feeling?"

"Dreadful, and weak as a kitten," the man in the bed told him. "How long have I been out?"

"A week," Baird said. "Do you want to know about it, or shall I come back later?"

He handed Armstrong a glass of iced water. Armstrong drained it gratefully, then lay back on his pillows and closed his eyes.

"Tell me," he said. "I want to know."

"It's pretty bad," Baird said quietly. "We reckon we got about twenty of them, but they got nineteen of our chaps too, not counting six Swordfish flying from Trincomalee to Minneriya; the Zeros shot the lot down."

"What about our chaps? Did we lose any of the old hands?"

Baird hesitated before replying. "We lost Eamonn O'Day. The Japs sent in some high-level bombers and he turned back to engage them. He called in to say he'd run out of fuel and that he was ditching, and that was the last we heard of him. We mounted a search, but there was no trace."

"Oh, Lord. Poor old Eamonn. Who else?"

Baird reeled off as many of the names as he could recall, feeling guilty that he could not remember those belonging to some of the later arrivals. There had been no time to become acquainted with them. Then he told Armstrong as much as he knew about the events of the past few days, although Armstrong's mind kept wandering as his friend spoke, and it would be some time before he knew the full story.

The Easter Sunday attack had caused considerable damage to built-up areas in Colombo, but thanks to determined fighter opposition the raiders had lost their cohesion and the damage to the port installations and shipping had been relatively light, although the auxiliary cruiser *Hector* and the destroyer *Tenedos* were sunk.

There were greater tragedies to come. At about noon, the cruisers *Cornwall* and *Dorsetshire* were sighted by a reconnaissance aircraft from the heavy cruiser *Tone*, and fifty-three Aichi D3A dive-bombers were immediately sent out to attack them. The bombing was devastatingly accurate and both ships were sunk. Over 1,100 men out of a total of about 1,500 were rescued later by the cruiser HMS *Enterprise* and two destroyers. Albacores from the *Indomitable* later made a night radar search for the enemy force, but it had withdrawn to the south-east to refuel before heading back north to strike at Trincomalee naval base.

At this time Admiral Somerville's Force A was steaming towards Ceylon from Addu Atoll, with his slow division (Force B) a long way behind; his ships were at times only 200 nautical miles from Nagumo's task force, but neither side made contact with the other, so Somerville, unable to locate the enemy, turned back towards his base to safeguard it against a possible surprise attack.

On 8 April a Catalina once again established contact with the Japanese carrier force 400 nautical miles to the east of Ceylon and the ships at Trincomalee were ordered to put to sea. All units – including the light carrier *Hermes* – were able to get clear before the expected attack by ninety-one high-level and dive-bombers, escorted by thirty-eight Zeros, developed early on the ninth. Of the twenty-three Hurricane and Fulmar fighters sent up to defend the harbour, nine were shot down, as were five out of a formation of nine Blenheim bombers sent out to try to locate the enemy force.

Only light damage was inflicted on the target, but on the way back to their carriers the Japanese aircrews sighted several ships, including the *Hermes*, the Australian destroyer *Vampire*, the corvette *Hollyhock* and two tankers. Three hours later, eighty dive-bombers arrived on the scene and sank all three warships and the tankers about sixty-five miles from Trincomalee. The *Hermes*, which had no aircraft on board, radioed desperately for help, but the surviving fighters at Trincomalee were in no position to offer it.

Armstrong must have slept, for when his eyes focused on the figure sitting beside his bed it was no longer Baird, but Kalinski.

"Stan!" Armstrong levered his top half upright with some difficulty; he felt much refreshed, but he was still horribly weak. "What have you being doing to yourself?"

He had noticed that Kalinski's right leg was in plaster from knee to toe.

"I had a little misunderstanding with a Zero," the Polish pilot said wryly. "A collision, to be exact. I lost my tail, and so decided that it was time for my Hurricane and I to part company. I landed right in the middle of Kandy, in the courtyard of some temple. It was full of people praying to a religious relic. Anyway, I was trying to steer clear of them when I hit a wall and broke my leg."

"Every cloud has a silver lining," Armstrong said. "After all, you might have broken your neck. The Tooth Relic was obviously looking after you. I'll tell you about that some time."

Kalinski looked at Armstrong as though the latter had gone crazy, and was about to say something when Philippa Windrush came in, carrying a tray. Kalinski mumbled something, nodded to her and made himself scarce as fast as his crutches would allow him. Armstrong wondered what was wrong.

"Soup," she said brusquely. "And just in case you're wondering why your friend made a rather undignified exit just then, it's because he's embarrassed. I must tell you that you can be rather verbose in your moments of delirium. Now, I don't mind it if you pour out your feelings for

195

me in private, but when two or three of your friends are present . . . well!"

"Oh, God," Armstrong muttered. "I say, Philippa, I'm really sorry."

She placed the tray on his lap and sat on the edge of the bed while she rearranged his pillows.

"Don't be a clot," she said gently. "I'm having you moved to a convalescent home up in the hills, and I'm coming with you. They've given me a few days' leave. You don't think I'm going to let you out of my sight again, do you? I think we have some serious talking to do. And call me Pip. I hate Philippa."

She touched him lightly on the cheek and got up. "Eat your soup", she ordered. "Let's get your strength up."

At the door she paused and looked back at him. She was wearing her crooked smile, and he thought he could detect a mischievous twinkle in her eye.

"I shall want to ask you lots and lots of questions about yourself," she said. "One in particular. Who's Phyllis?"

She was gone before she had time to see a spoonful of soup cascade down Armstrong's pyjama front.

Sixteen

From a distance there seemed to be nothing unusual about the small group of warships plunging through the waters of the Pacific 700 miles east of Japan. It was a fairly typical US Navy task force, with two aircraft carriers screened by their watchful escort of cruisers and destroyers.

Close to, however, it became apparent that there was something very unusual about one of the carriers – or, more accurately, about the aircraft ranged on her flight deck. These were no Navy machines, but something much larger and more powerful: North American B-25 Mitchell bombers of the Army Air Force.

The date was 18 April 1942. The carrier was the USS *Hornet*; she formed part of Task Force 16 under the command of Vice-Admiral W.F. Halsey, and in just a few hours' time she would launch her B-25s on one of the most audacious missions in the history of air warfare: the first ever air strike on Tokyo.

The plan was conceived initially in a small way in January 1942, as America still reeled from the shock of Pearl Harbor, by Captain Francis Low, an officer on the staff of the US Navy Commander-in-Chief Captain Ernest King. He had been to inspect work on the new attack carrier USS Hornet, commissioned in the previous October, and had watched with interest as the pilots of her air group practised deck landings and take-offs on a 500-foot strip marked out on an airfield adjacent to the shipyard.

Low had been wondering for some time about the possibility of carrying out an air strike on Japan. To use ordinary carrier aircraft would be out of the question; their range was not great enough, and any task force would have to sail almost to within sight of the enemy coast before launching an attack. But suppose, thought Low, that the Army had a bomber with sufficient range, and the ability to take off in 500 feet with a load of fuel and bombs on board – then why not put a few of them on a carrier like the Hornet, and hit targets on the Japanese mainland?

He put the idea to Admiral King, who instructed him to discuss it with the air officer on his staff, Captain Donald Duncan, and present a full report on its feasibility. Duncan was enthusiastic, and immediately got to work on some facts and figures. An experienced pilot himself, he quickly realised that only one aircraft type might be suitable: the B-25 Mitchell medium bomber.

Powered by two 1,700-horsepower Wright Cyclone engines, the first B-25 had flown in August 1940, the design having been ordered straight 'off the drawing board' in September 1939. The latest version, the B-25B, was well armed with machine guns in dorsal, ventral and tail turrets, and could carry up to 3,000 pounds of bombs over a range of 1,300 miles. Its top speed was 300 miles per hour at 15,000 feet, and it carried a crew of five. However, the B-25B needed at least 1,250 feet of runway to take off safely with a 2,000-pound bomb load; whether it could be made light enough to take off in only 500 feet remained to be seen.

Inside a week, Duncan's feasibility study, fifty pages long, was on Admiral King's desk. King read through it and at once telephoned General Henry Arnold, the Army Air Force C-in-C, to arrange a meeting. 'Hap' Arnold had become one of the first American military pilots back in 1911 and had always fought hard, sometimes at the risk of his career, to make the United States a strong air power. He was greatly impressed by the scheme and agreed to send three B-25s to Norfolk, Virginia, so that their take-off characteristics could be tested with various load configurations.

During the next few days, it was found to everyone's amazement that a stripped-down, lightly loaded B-25 could actually take off well within the 500 feet that represented a carrier's deck length. Captain Duncan had already recommended that the USS *Hornet*, commanded by the able and talented Captain Marc Mitscher, should be the carrier used in the operation, and one day late in January 1942 she put to sea with a single B-25 on board. Thirty miles offshore, with the carrier steaming into wind, the B-25 pilot took the bomber roaring down the flight deck, lifted her into the air with a 150 feet to spare, and flew back to Norfolk.

Meanwhile, General Arnold had been giving a great

deal of thought to the man he would select to organise and lead the operation. He needed a man with tremendous organisational ability; a man who was a highly experienced pilot; and one, moreover, who had the engineering expertise necessary to supervise the technical modifications that would have to be made to the B-25s.

One man, among all the potential candidates, met every criterion admirably. He was Lieutenant-Colonel James H. Doolittle, one of the leading pioneers of American aviation. He had learned to fly with the US Army in 1918, and in the years after the First World War his flying career had been marked by a number of notable 'firsts'. He had become the first man to span the American continent with a flight from Florida to California; the first American to pilot an aircraft with reference only to instruments from take-off to landing; the first American to perform an outside loop; and in 1925 he had won the coveted Schneider Trophy for the United States. He had also been a test pilot for the Army Air Corps, had demonstrated American fighter designs overseas, and – of vital importance to this new assignment – he had obtained the degree of a Doctor of Science in aeronautical engineering at the Massachusetts Institute of Technology.

Jimmy Doolittle had recently retired from Shell when he was recalled to military service in 1940. He was forty-five years old, at the peak of his aviation career, and yet he welcomed the chance to get back into uniform. During those months of 1940 and 1941, he sensed that America would soon be in the war, and he was keen to play his part.

During 1941 General Arnold, who was an old friend, used him as a kind of trouble-shooter to deal with the hundreds of problems that arose as the US aircraft industry strove to gear up its resources to meet the growing demand for modern aircraft by the armed forces. This was still his job when Arnold summoned him to Washington and gave him first details of the daring scheme to bomb Japan.

Like Captain Duncan, Doolittle realised at once that the B-25 was the only suitable aircraft. The problem was to strip it down so that it could take off from the carrier with a sizeable load of fuel and bombs, while not impairing its performance in any way. He made a lot of calculations, which he submitted to Arnold, and the C-in-C told him to get on with the job of modifying the bombers and training their crews while Duncan set up the whole operation and arranged full co-operation between Navy and Air Force – not the easiest of tasks at the best of times.

While Duncan set off for Pearl Harbor to brief Admiral Chester Nimitz, C-in-C United States Pacific Fleet, who would be responsible for getting a task force together, Doolittle assembled a team of engineers and took a B-25 apart. He removed the ventral gun turret and installed a rubber 60-gallon fuel tank in its place, and another rubber tank holding 160 gallons was fitted into the cat-walk above the bomb-bay. Together with the existing fuel tanks, that made a total of 1,050 gallons. He also removed the top-secret Norden bombsight and replaced it with much cheaper and more rudimentary equipment; the attack was going to be made from low level, and Doolittle reckoned that the sophistication of the Norden would not be necessary. Quite apart from that, no one wanted the new sight to fall into enemy hands. New propellers and de-icing equipment were also fitted, while every weighty item – including radios – that was thought to be not absolutely vital was removed.

After ten days of modifications and trials, Doolittle found himself able to lift a stripped-down B-25 from a 400-foot length of runway while carrying 2,000 pounds of bombs and a full fuel load. While modifications to more B-25s went ahead, General Arnold authorised Doolittle to select his crews, and advised him to draw them from the Air Force's most experienced B-25 units: the 17th Bomb Group and the 89th Reconnaissance Squadron, both based on Columbia Field, South Carolina.

Doolittle flew to Columbia early in February and selected twenty-four crews, all of them volunteers. A week later they reported to Eglin Field, near Pensacola in Florida, where they began intensive training with the modified B-25s. They still had not been told the nature of the target, but by this time some of them were making intelligent guesses. Time and again, as the rumours began to fly, Doolittle stressed the need for secrecy. The success of their mission, and their lives, depended on it.

While training continued, the naval task force was taking shape. It was to consist of the carriers *Hornet* and *Enterprise*, two heavy cruisers, two light cruisers, eight destroyers and two tankers, and it was to be commanded by Vice-Admiral 'Bull' Halsey. He flew to San Francisco, where he met Doolittle, and went over the details of the plan. He was able to clear up one thing that had been bothering Doolittle: whether they would have to push their aircraft unceremoniously over the side if they were attacked, leaving room for *Hornet*'s air squadrons to come on deck and go into action, or whether they would have time to fly off. Halsey told them that they would probably be able to take off and fly to Midway Island if the attack took place outside Japanese waters; after that, with Midway out of range, they could either ditch their B-25's overboard or take off for Japan as planned, with the prospect of coming down in the China Sea after the raid. If all went well, *Hornet* would take them as close as possible – but not within 400 miles – of the Japanese coast, giving them a sufficient fuel margin to reach China after the attack.

By the middle of March 1942 Doolittle's crews had completed their training, achieving astonishing standards of skill. One pilot succeeded in taking off after a run of only 287 feet. They now flew down to McClelland Field near Sacramento, California, where the final maintenance checks were to be made. Afterwards, they took their bombers to Alameda Naval Station, near San Francisco, where they finally made rendezvous with their carrier.

Doolittle had decided to take sixteen B-25s on the *Hornet*, and getting them on board was a complicated business. Carrier air groups normally fly on when their ships are at sea, but there could be no question of this with the B-25s. They had to be lifted aboard with cranes, and then lashed to the flight deck. They did not have folding wings, like naval aircraft, which ruled out any possibility of their being stowed in the big hangar below decks. When the bombers were all on board the *Hornet* had a distinctly stern-heavy appearance, as though a cluster of huge parasites had suddenly descended on that part of her.

The *Hornet* sailed from Alameda on 2 April. Not until she had been at sea for twenty-four hours did Doolittle brief the crews who had been selected to fly the mission; until now not even his second-in-command, Major Jack Hilger of the 89th Reconnaissance Squadron, had known the specific nature of the target – or rather targets, for the B-25s were to hit Yokohama, Osaka, Kobe and Nagoya as well as Tokyo. Every day, during the remainder of the voyage, the crews spent long hours poring over the bulky target-intelligence folders which Doolittle, Low and Duncan had assembled. Before long the layout of their objectives, together with the nature of the terrain they would have to fly over to reach them, was as familiar as the cockpits of their bombers.

The *Hornet* rendezvoused with the other warships of Task Force 16 north of the Hawaiian Islands, and sailed straight on across the Pacific towards the launching-point. At dawn on 18 April, the day fixed for the strike, the vessels were still 700 miles from the Japanese coast and the weather was worsening, with a high sea running and the wind strength increasing all the time. Adding to all the other worries, a small Japanese ship was sighted at 0630 hours, and although the cruiser *Northampton* was quickly sent off to blow her out of the water, it was certain that if she carried radio she would have had ample time to signal the task force's presence – unless her crew had mistaken the warships for their own.

Doolittle's original plan had been to take off some time ahead of the others and drop four clusters of incendiary bombs on Tokyo just before nightfall, starting a blaze that would lead the following B-25s straight to the target. Now, because of that chance encounter with the Japanese steamer, everything had to be altered. With the possibility that Japanese bombers might even now be preparing to take off to attack the task force, Admiral Halsey could not afford to endanger his ships by holding course until they reached the planned launch point, 300 miles further on. The take-off would have to be brought forward by several hours, and the crews all knew what that meant. Even with full tanks, the bombers might not have enough fuel to reach China.

Then Jimmy Doolittle hit on a scheme that would help alleviate the fuel problem. He ordered ten five-gallon drums of petrol to be loaded on each aircraft, and told the crew chiefs to use them to top up the ventral fuel tank as its level dropped during the flight. Immediately afterwards, Doolittle summoned all the pilots to a last-minute briefing, in which he emphasised the take-off procedure. The *Hornet* was battling her way into the teeth of a thirty-five-knot gale and she was pitching violently, so it was vital that the pilots started their take-off run at exactly the right moment, otherwise they would find themselves taking off uphill or diving into the sea.

The crews filed out to their aircraft and climbed aboard. All eyes were on Doolittle's B-25 as its pilot opened the throttles slowly, holding the bomber against the brakes. The bow of the carrier dipped sharply, then began to rise, and at that moment Doolittle released his brakes and gave the engines full power. The B-25 began to move, slowly at first, then gathering speed. With a hundred feet to spare Doolittle lifted her cleanly away from the deck and took her up in a steep climb, turning and bringing her round in a tight circle, flying over the length of the carrier before setting course. There was a reason for this; the bombers' compasses had been affected by the metal mass of the carrier, so by flying over her while Captain Mitscher held a westerly heading the pilots could check the accuracy of their instruments.

All sixteen B-25s took off safely, despite the heaving motion of the carrier, and followed Doolittle's bomber in the direction of Japan. The second B-25 to take off, flown by Lieutenant Travis Hoover, formed up with Doolittle and the two machines flew on together. They had 670 miles to go to Tokyo, and for the next four and a half hours there was little to do but hold a steady course, flying at the slowest possible economic cruising speed in order to conserve fuel. Doolittle took turns at sharing the controls with his co-pilot, Lieutenant Richard Cole. The other members of his crew were the navigator, Lieutenant Henry Potter, the bombardier, Sergeant Fred Braemer, and the crew chief, Sergeant Paul J. Leonard, who also doubled up as gunner.

They stayed low, as low as 200 feet above the sea. Although the Japanese air defences were not thought to have the benefit of radar, the lower the vessels remained, the less the risk of detection by surface vessels or patrol aircraft.

At 1330 hours, Jimmy Doolittle sighted the enemy coast. Potter told him that they would make landfall thirty miles north of Tokyo, and he turned out to be dead right. As they crossed the coast, Doolittle picked up a large lake over on the left, and a quick check with the map confirmed his navigator's accuracy. He turned south, skimming low over a patchwork of fields. Peasants looked up and waved, mistaking the speeding B-25 for one of their own aircraft. Once, Doolittle looked up and saw five Japanese fighters, cruising a couple of thousand feet above, but they made no move to attack and eventually turned away. Another good point about this low-level work was that the B-25's olive-drab camouflage blended in nicely with the background, making the bombers extremely difficult to spot from aircraft flying at a higher altitude.

The bombers thundered on, skirting the slopes of hills, leapfrogging high-tension cables. There was no flak; it was just like one of the many training flights back home. Suddenly, dead ahead, was the great sprawling complex of the Japanese capital city, and Doolittle took the B-25 up to 1,500 feet. In the glazed nose, bombardier Fred Braemer peered ahead, searching for the munitions factory that was their target. He found it and steered Doolittle towards it, the pilot holding the aircraft rock-steady in response to the bombardier's instructions. On Doolittle's instrument panel a red light blinked four times, each blink denoting the release of an incendiary cluster. The B-25 jumped, lightened of its 2,000-pound load, and Doolittle opened the throttles wide, anxious to get clear of the target area.

The flight across Tokyo lasted five minutes. Not until

they were over the outer suburbs did flak burst across the sky, far in their wake. There was no time to observe the results of their attack; it was full throttle all the way to the coast, their ground speed aided by a twenty-five knot tail wind.

Behind Doolittle, the fifteen other B-25s were attacking their assigned targets. Travis Hoover released his bombs and fled, following much the same route as Doolittle, while at Yokohama Lieutenant Edgar E. McElroy, who had been the thirteenth pilot to take off, had an extraordinary stroke of luck. His target was the docks area, and right in the middle of it was a Ryujo-class aircraft carrier. McElroy dropped a 500-pound bomb slap on the flight deck, causing damage that put the ship out of action for several weeks. He and his crew got away safely.

Other crews were not so lucky. Lieutenant William G. Farrow hit oil storage tanks and an aircraft factory in the Osaka-Kobe area, got away unscathed, flew to China and baled out with the rest of his crew in bad weather, only to be captured by pro-Japanese Chinese and turned over to the enemy. He and another crew member, Corporal C. Spatz, were murdered; the other three spent the rest of the war in prison camps.

The B-25 flown by Lieutenant Dean Hallmark also reached China and the crew baled out over Poyang Lake. Two crew members, Sergeant William Deiter and Corporal Donald Fitzmorris, landed in the lake and were drowned; Dean Hallmark was captured and killed in cold blood; his co-pilot, Lieutenant Robert Meder, died of starvation in prison camp. The sole survivor of Hallmark's crew was the navigator, Lieutenant Chase Neilson, who spent forty months as a prisoner of war.

Some crews had lucky escapes. Lieutenant Richard O. Joyce, the pilot of the sixteenth B-25, was attacked by nine Zero fighters over Tokyo. Their fire ripped a great gash in the bomber's rear fuselage and fragments peppered the tail, but despite this Joyce succeeded in getting away and baled out with his men over friendly Chinese territory. Another pilot, Ross Greening, was also attacked by fighters; his gunner, Sergeant Melville Carter, shot down one of them and Greening got away. He and his crew also baled out over China, suffering only minor injuries on landing.

The plan was for all the B-25s to head south-west across the China Sea, skirting the Japanese islands of Shikoku and Kyushu, and fly to the Chinese airfield of Chuchow in Chekiang province. The plan, however, was badly disrupted by the weather. First of all, as Jimmy Doolittle found during the sea crossing, the wind veered, reducing the bombers' ground speed and using up more precious fuel; and then, when they crossed the Chinese coast, they found a thick blanket of cloud stretching as far as the eye could see. Doolittle had been promised that a homing beacon would have been set up at Chuchow, but they could detect no welcoming radio signal from it. In fact, the aircraft carrying it to the field had crashed in the mountains, and it later transpired that the message alerting the Chinese to expect the American bombers had somehow gone astray, so that no one knew they were coming.

Not daring to risk a descent through the murk – there

were mountains all around Chuchow, and by this time it was dark – Doolittle ordered his crew to bale out. They were picked up by Chinese troops and eventually arrived at Chuchow to find five aircraft captains – Major Jack Hilger and Lieutenants Ross Greening, David Jones, William Bower and Robert Gray – already there, together with their crews. Baling out, they had sustained one casualty; Gray's gunner, Corporal Leland D. Faktor, who had been killed when he fractured his skull on landing.

Considering that Chuchow was surrounded on three sides by Japanese forces, it seemed incredible that only two crews, Farrow's and Hallmark's, had actually had the misfortune to land in enemy territory. In the twenty-four hours after the raid, reports began to trickle in about the fate of the others. Captain David Jones, Lieutenant Everett Holstrom and their crews were all safe; Lieutenant Ted Lawson had ditched off the coast despite a badly injured leg and he and his men had struggled ashore, where they were sheltered by Chinese guerrillas. Lawson, however, lost his leg. Lieutenant Harold F. Watson and his crew had baled out about one hundred miles south of Poyang Lake; Watson had suffered a broken arm, but no one else was injured. Lieutenant Donald Smith had landed not far from Lawson, and it was one of his crew – Lieutenant T.R. White, the only medical officer on the flight – who had amputated the injured pilot's leg under appallingly primitive conditions.

That left only Captain Edward J. York unaccounted for, and it was some time before Doolittle learned what had become of him. After bombing Tokyo and heading out to sea, York had discovered that his B-25 had used up far more fuel than should have been the case, and there was no possibility of reaching China. He had therefore turned north and landed on Russian territory forty miles north of Vladivostok. He and his crew were interned, and it was only after more than a year of protracted negotiations that the Russians released them.

Of the eighty men who took part in the raid, ten died and fifteen more were injured, in some cases only slightly. Sadly, twelve of Doolittle's gallant band were to die later in the war. Doolittle himself was promoted to the rank of brigadier-general immediately after the raid and awarded the Medal of Honor. All the other survivors received the Distinguished Flying Cross. Doolittle later commanded the United States Twelfth Air Force in North Africa and the Eighth Air Force in England.

Although most of the targets assigned to the B-25 crews had been hit, the damage caused had been slight, mainly because the aircraft had carried relatively light bomb loads. The effect on the morale of the Japanese, however, flushed and made cocksure by their recent victories, was incalculable. There was also another consequence, and it was to turn the tide of the war against Japan.

Epilogue

Admiral Yamamoto's Flagship: 10 June 1942

Admiral Isoroku Yamamoto, Commander-in-Chief of the Imperial Japanese Navy, stared moodily at the huge wall map of the Pacific Ocean and wondered why things had begun to go wrong. His plan, after all, had been a masterly one.

He was determined that never again would American aircraft bomb Japan, and that meant expanding the boundaries of Japan's Pacific conquests. The first step was to secure the whole of New Guinea, which could then be used as a stepping-stone for a full-scale invasion of Australia.

Upon his signal, Admiral Nagumo's carrier force had been withdrawn from the Indian Ocean two days after the audacious American air attack on Japan, just as Nagumo was preparing for another assault on Ceylon. Three of his carriers had been detached to act as a covering force for a Japanese landing at Port Moresby, the vital port that sustained the Allied troops fighting in the steaming New Guinea jungle.

For a week, early in May, the Japanese and the Allies had hurled their dive-bombers and torpedo-bombers at one another's ships in what the Americans and Australians called the Battle of the Coral Sea. It was the first time in history that opposing naval forces had fought an engagement without the warships making contact.

Japanese attempts at landing troops had been thwarted by air attacks, which had sunk several vessels. The light carrier *Shohu* had also been sunk, and the fleet carrier *Shokaku* heavily damaged. Then the Japanese had hit back hard, sinking an American destroyer and fleet oiler and, most importantly, the aircraft carrier *Lexington*, which exploded after being hit by torpedoes.

The result had been a tactical victory for the Japanese but a strategic one for the Allies, for the planned amphibious assault on Port Moresby had had to be called off.

Worse, much worse, had followed. As the Japanese recoiled from Port Moresby, a second strong thrust took place in the central Pacific. Heavy units of the Battle Fleet, led by Nagumo's other four carriers, had sailed for the island of Midway, which was first to be neutralised by air strikes and then occupied by Japanese marines.

Yamamoto suddenly swung round on his heel and faced the man who stood behind him. He was three years older than Chuichi Nagumo, yet he seemed much younger. Recent events had aged Nagumo beyond belief.

"From your own lips, Nagumo. I want to hear it from your own lips."

Nagumo swallowed. His face was an impassive mask, but there were tears in his eyes.

"The attack began as planned, sir. Six days ago, the Task Force launched one hundred and eight aircraft against Midway. At the same time, American aircraft attempted to attack our Task Force. They secured no hits, and we destroyed seventeen of them. I then received reports that an American Task Force was approaching, but the reports were confusing and I did not decide to deploy my aircraft against it until too late. Sir, I humbly apologise for this error."

Nagumo bowed slightly. Yamamoto knew what the apology had cost him. He also knew what Nagumo's omission had cost the Imperial Navy. "Go on," he ordered.

"Sir, we were then attacked by two waves of aircraft, both torpedo-bombers and dive-bombers. They were from the enemy carriers identified as the *Enterprise, Hornet* and *Yorktown*. Our defending fighters concentrated on the torpedo-bombers.

"There were forty-one of them in all, and thirty-five were shot down. Then the dive-bombers, which had made a wide detour in order to attack from an unexpected direction, fell on the *Akagi, Kaga* and *Soryu*." Nagumo hesitated for a few moments, as though marshalling his thoughts, then continued:

"The dive-bombers got in unimpeded because our fighters had not yet had time to regain altitude after intercepting the torpedo-bombers. Consequently, it may be said that the American dive-bombers' success was made possible by the martyrdom of their torpedo planes.

"The *Akagi* had taken two direct hits. From the bridge, I could also see that *Kaga* and *Soryu* had also been hit and were giving off heavy columns of black smoke. It was a horrible scene. On *Akagi*, the fires quickly spread among the aircraft ranged on deck, ready to take off, and their torpedoes began to explode, making it impossible to bring the fires under control. Because of the spreading fires, our general loss of combat efficiency and disruption of communications, it was no longer possible for me to exercise control over the remainder of the Task Force, and I was persuaded to transfer my flag to the light cruiser *Nagara*."

Tears welled up in Nagumo's eyes again. He had hated to leave behind the men with whom he had shared every joy and sorrow of the war. He remembered Captain Aoki's last words to him, begging him to leave the stricken carrier. "Admiral, I will take care of the ship. Please, we all implore you, move your flag to the *Nagara* and resume command of the Task Force."

Poor Aoki, gone now. Along with Captain Akada of the Kaga and Yanagimoto of the *Soryu*. And Rear-Admiral Yamaguchi and Captain Kaku of the *Hiryu*, too, for she had been attacked by air groups from the American carriers *Enterprise* and *Hornet*, set on fire and abandoned. It was small consolation that *Hiryu*'s aircraft had hit the carrier *Yorktown* with torpedoes and bombs, and that she had been finished off later by a submarine.

If only I had launched my strike aircraft a few minutes earlier, Nagumo whispered inwardly, almost beside himself with misery and grief.

Yamamoto had turned away and was once again looking at the map, but without really seeing it. In a single day he had lost three quarters of his carrier strength. Other carriers were being built in Japan, but they would not be ready. Not in time to restore command of the air over the Pacific.

He had a sudden terrible vision of his beloved homeland in flames, razed from end to end by American bombers flying from bases that crept ever closer to Japan. And there pounded through his brain a thought he found impossible to dismiss.

For the Allies, the Battle of Midway marked the end of the beginning.

For Japan, it marked the beginning of the end.

NEATH PORT TALBOT LIBRARY
AND INFORMATION SERVICES

1	6/04	25		49		73	
2		26		50		74	
3		27		51		75	
4	1/03	28		52		76	
5		29		53		77	
6		30		54		78	
7	5/01	31		55		79	
8	3/2000	32		56		80	
9		33		57		81	
10	9/08	34		58		82	
11		35		59		83	
12		36		60		84	
13		37		61		85	
14		38		62		86	
15		39		63		87	
16		40		64		88	
17		41		65		89	
18		42		66		90	
19		43		67		91	
20		44		68		92	
21		45		69		COMMUNITY SERVICES	
22		46		70			
23		47		71		NPT/111	
24		48		72			